Alphonse de Lamartine, Richard Henry Stoddard, George Sand, Prosper Mérim[illegible] Herbert

Prosper Mérimée's Letters to an Incognita

outlook

Alphonse de Lamartine, Richard Henry Stoddard, George Sand, Prosper Mérimée, Mary Elizabeth Herbert

Prosper Mérimée's Letters to an Incognita

Reprint of the original, first published in 1875.

1st Edition 2024 | ISBN: 978-3-38538-414-9

Verlag (Publisher): Outlook Verlag GmbH, Zeilweg 44, 60439 Frankfurt, Deutschland
Vertretungsberechtigt (Authorized to represent): E. Roepke, Zeilweg 44, 60439 Frankfurt, Deutschland
Druck (Print): Books on Demand GmbH, In de Tarpen 42, 22848 Norderstedt, Deutschland

Bric-a-Brac Series

PROSPER MERIMEE'S

LETTERS TO AN INCOGNITA

WITH RECOLLECTIONS BY

LAMARTINE AND GEORGE SAND

EDITED BY

RICHARD HENRY STODDARD

NEW YORK
SCRIBNER, ARMSTRONG, AND COMPANY
1875

CONTENTS.

PREFACE.

LAMARTINE, MÉRIMÉE, and GEORGE SAND have added such brilliancy to the French literature of the present century, that their association in this volume is entirely natural and calls for no explanation or justification. Alphonse de Lamartine was born at Mâcon on the Saone, on the 21st of October, 1792, and died in February, 1869; Prosper Mérimée was born in Paris in 1803, and died in Cannes, September 23, 1870; George Sand (Madame Dudevant, whose maiden name was Amantine Lucile Aurore Dupin) was born in Paris on July 1st, 1804; and happily, the date of her death cannot yet be named. The extraordinary brilliancy of the literary reputation of Lamartine, conjoined with the great influence which he at one time exerted in French politics, make him unquestionably the most prominent of the trio. The financial embarrassments in which his extravagant habits plunged him toward the close of his life, placed him in such an unfortunate attitude toward those who had for many years flattered and petted him, that his great popularity suffered a disastrous eclipse; but the matchless eloquence which he repeatedly displayed as an orator, the influence which he now and then possessed as a statesman, and the poetic glow and fervor which breathe through all his writings, have secured for him and his works a repu tation and a name which must endure. The wide diversity in the character of the writings of George Sand makes it difficult as yet to assign her a precise place in literature, but some of her works will live as long as the language in which they were written. Both Lamartine and George Sand are nearly as well known to Americans as they are to their own countrymen. For nearly the last half century their names have been widely familiar, and the facts of their respective careers are easily accessible. Until recently, however, Mérimée has been but slightly known, save to his own countrymen. He first appeared before the public in 1825, as the translator from the Spanish of several dramas, under the title "Théâtre de Clara Gazul;" in 1833, he published a moral tale, "The Double Mistake" ("La Double Méprise"), and then there followed at intervals, notes of journeys in the South, and also in the West of France, "Stories in Roman History;" "A History of Don Pedro I., King of Castile;" "An Episode in the History of Russia," etc., etc. "Columba," a novel which was published in 1841, was extremely successful, and upon this, more than upon any other of his works, his popular reputation will probably rest. Whether that reputation can be permanent among his own countrymen is a question which it is hardly worth while to discuss. In the course of his career, however, first as Inspector-General of Historical Monuments, a position to which he was appointed as early as 1834, then as member of the French Academy, with an election to which he was honored in 1844, and afterwards as Senator (1853), he saw French society in all its phases and constantly under circumstances which gave him the most excellent opportunities for observation. Cynical by nature, the lingering disease to which he finally yielded, led him to look at men and things, especially during all the later years of his life, in a morbidly critical way; but that he was capable of loving ardently, these now famous "Letters to an Incognita" abundantly prove. Indeed, they show something even more remarkable than this; that the lover could settle down into the devoted friend, maintaining during a period of over thirty years,—for this singular correspondence extends from 1842 to 1870,—the sincerest admiration for the woman for whom, at one time, Mérimée cherished something more than a Platonic affection. As regards the identity of the "Incognita" and the manner in which the publication of these letters was received in Paris, it is enough to quote the opening paragraphs from a paper suggested by them, which appeared in the "London Quarterly Review" for January, 1874. The writer says: "No literary event since the war, has excited anything like such a sensation in Paris, as the publication of the "Letters à une Inconnue." Even politics became a secondary consideration for the hour, and Academicians or Deputies of opposite parties, might be seen eagerly accosting each other in the chamber or the street, to inquire who this fascinating and perplexing unknown could be. The statement in the "Revue des Deux Mondes" that she was an Englishwoman, moving in brilliant society, was not supported by evidence; and M. Blanchard, the painter from whom the publisher received the manuscripts, died, most provokingly, at the very commencement of the inquiry, and made no sign. Some intimate friends of Mérimée, rendered incredulous by wounded self-love at not having been admitted to his confidence, insisted that there was no secret to tell; their hypothesis being, that the "Incognita" was a myth, and the letters a romance, with which some petty details of actual life had been interwoven (as in "Gulliver's Travels" or "Robinson Crusoe"), to keep up the mystification. But an artist like Mérimée would not have left his work in so unformed a state, so defaced by repetitions, or with such a want of proportion between the parts. With the evidence before us as we write, we incline to the belief that the lady was French by birth, and during the early years of the correspondence in the position of *dame de compagnie* or travelling companion to a Madame M—— de B——, who passes in the letters under the pseudonym of Lady M——. It appears from one of them that she inherited a fortune in 1843; and she has been constantly identified with a respectable single lady residing in Paris with two nieces, and a character for pedantry fastened on her (perhaps unjustly), on the strength of the Greek which she learned from Mérimée."

As regards Mérimée himself, it is only necessary to quote some passages from the "Study," with which the distinguished author Henri Taine prefaces these "Letters to an Incognita." He writes: "I frequently met Mérimée in society — a tall, erect, pale man, who, excepting his smile, had very much the appearance of an Englishman; at least he possessed that cold, distant air that in advance repels all familiarity. One was impressed, merely on seeing him, with his natural or acquired phlegm, his self-control, his habit and determination of holding himself in perfect check. His countenance, especially on ceremonious occasions, was impassible even in intimate circles, and when recounting some drollery his voice remained even and calm, never any outburst nor enthusiasm; while he related the raciest details in fitting words with the tone of a man asking for a cup of tea.

He so strenuously subdued all manifestations of sensibility as to seem destitute of it; but it was not so, indeed quite the reverse; as there are racers so well broken in by their master, that once well in hand they no longer indulge in a caracole. This training began at an early period with Mérimée; for he was but ten years old when, having committed some slight fault, he was severely reprimanded and sent from the room: and weeping, overcome with distress, he had just closed the door, when he heard a burst of laughter, and some one said: 'Poor child, he really thought us angry.' He revolted at the idea of being deceived; he swore to repress thenceforth so humiliating a sensitiveness, and he kept his word. 'Remember to distrust,' was his motto. To guard against impulse, ardor, and enthusiasm, never entirely to allow himself full play, to maintain always a personal reserve, to be the dupe neither of others nor of himself, to act and write as if perpetually in the presence of an indifferent and mocking spectator, — such was the salient feature which, graven more and more deeply into his nature, left its imprint on every phase of his life, his work, and his talent. He lived as an amateur; and indeed, possessed of a critical taste and habit, one can hardly do otherwise; by dint of reversing the tapestry, one ends by looking habitually at the wrong side, seeing instead of handsome personages in fine attitudes, only bits of thread. Early in life, Mérimée possessed a competency, afterwards a congenial and interesting office, that of Inspector-General of Historical Monuments, and subsequently a place in the Senate and a position at court. He was competent, active, and useful in regard to the monuments; in the Senate he had the good taste to be generally absent or silent; while at court he preserved his independence and freedom of speech. To travel, study, observe, to dissect men and events, formed his chief occupation, his official bonds holding him in but slight restraint. A man of such wit as Mérimée possessed, is necessarily held in a certain respect, his irony transpiercing the finest chain-mail of his adversaries. It would be difficult to present a more serious deportment in corporate assemblies, and to entertain less internal respect for them, than Mérimée exhibited. Grave, dignified, studied in attitude, his manners were irreproachable when he visited the Academy or improvised a public discourse; nevertheless, with an occasional sly and comic touch that turned both orator and audience into ridicule. Two distinct personages existed in Mérimée; the one fulfilling with easy propriety the duties, and acquitting himself with grace in the splendors of society; the other holding himself apart and above his second half, whose performance he regarded with a bantering or resigned air; and so also there was a dual self in his ties of affection or sentiment. On the one hand a perfectly natural man, good and even tender, than whom no one was more loyal, unfailing in friendship, and who once having offered his hand, never withdrew it. This characteristic was strikingly shown in his defense of M. Libri against the judges of the court and public opinion; the action of a true knight who singly throws his gage of battle to a whole army. Condemned to fine and imprisonment, he did not assume the air of a martyr, but showed as much grace in submitting to the penalty of his ill-fortune, as bravery in provoking it; and made no mention of it, save with quiet humor, in a preface, saying that he 'had passed fortnight of July in a retreat, where he was in no wise incommoded by the sun, and where he enjoyed profound leisure.' He was obliging and earnest in serving others; and persons who, in begging his good offices, left him disconcerted by his cold manner, would be surprised by his appearance a month afterwards, having in his pocket an affirmative answer to their petition. In his correspondence a striking statement escapes him, which his friends find true, — 'It rarely chances that I sacrifice others to myself, but whenever it happens, I suffer all possible remorse.'

"Towards the close of his life two elderly English ladies were seen at his house, to whom he seldom spoke, and about whom he did not seem to trouble himself greatly; yet a friend saw tears in his eyes because one of them was ill. He never made any allusion to his deepest feelings; and here we have a correspondence, first lover-like, then merely friendly, that continued during thirty years, and yet the name of his correspondent is unknown! By those who read these letters aright, he will be found gracious, affectionate, delicate, earnestly in love, and, almost incredibly, at times a poet, even moved to superstition, like a lyrical German. But by the side of the lover, the critic still appears, and the conflict between these opposing forces in the same nature produces very singular effects; in such a case, however, it is wise not to scan too closely. 'Do you know,' says La Fontaine, 'that however slightly I may love, I no more see the defects of the one exciting the sentiment, than does a mole a hundred feet below the earth. With the sowing of the first grain of love, I never fail to surround it with my entire stock of incense.' In this, perhaps, lay the secret of his charm. In Mérimée's letters harsh words were showered with caresses. Tenderness, altercation, and reconciliation reigned successively: for he seems to have met a character as restive, as unyielding, and independent as his own, — *a lioness though tame.* After a violent quarrel, an affectionate word recalls him to her feet: and these alternations of love and anger finally subside into a calm and enduring friendship. They met at the Louvre, at Versailles, in the neighboring woods, took long clandestine walks together several times a week, even in January; he admired 'a radiant countenance, a subtle charm, a white hand, superb black hair,' an intelligence and attainments worthy of his own, the graces of an original beauty, the attractions of a comprehensive culture, the seductions of delicious toilet and skillful coquetry; he breathed the perfume of an education so choice, and 'a nature so refined, as to epitomize for him a rounded civilization;' in short, he was under the spell. The critic, however, in turn replaced the lover; he unraveled the meaning of a reply, of a gesture; he disengaged himself from sentiment, the better to judge a character; and wrote her rather biting truths and epigrams which were returned to him the following day.

"Such he was in life, and such we find him in his books. He studied and wrote as an amateur, passing from one subject to another, as fancy or occasion prompted, giving himself up to no science, using his talent for the illustration of no theory. This was the want neither of application nor capability; on the contrary, few men possessed more varied attainments. He was master of the Italian, Greek, Latin, Spanish, English, and Russian languages, with their history and literature: and I believe that he also read German. From time to time a phrase, a note shows the point to which he had pursued these studies. He spoke *Calo* in a manner to astonish the Spanish gypsies; he understood the various Spanish dialects, and deciphered ancient Catalonian charters, and scanned English poetry. Only they who have studied an entire literature in print and manuscript, during the four or five successive periods of the language, its style and orthography, can appreciate the facility and the perseverance necessary to enable one to understand Spanish so thoroughly as the author of 'Don Pedro;' and Russian as the writer of the 'Cosaques' and the 'Faux Démétrius.' He possessed a remarkable lingual gift, and acquired languages up to a ripe age, becoming a philologist towards the end of his life, applying himself at Cannes to the minutiæ of study pertaining to comparative grammar. To this knowledge of books he joined extensive learning respecting monuments, his reports proving him to be a specialist as to those of France, comprehending not only the effect but the technicalities of architecture. He studied each church on the spot, aided by the best architects; his memory of locality was excellently trained, and born of a family of painters, he had early handled the brush, being an artist in water-colors; in short, he investigated the subject exhaustively, and having a horror of specious phrases, touched no topic unless with certainty of detail. He travelled frequently; once in the East, twice in Greece, a dozen or fifteen times in England, in Spain, and elsewhere, studying the manners, not only of good company but of bad; consorting familiarly with gypsies and bull-fighters, and relating stories to the peasants beneath the Andalusian stars. Possessed of these varied acquirements, and of such noble faculties, Mérimée might easily have attained an eminent position, both in history and art; but as a historian he occupies only an average rank, while his place, though high, is but limited in art. Nearly always he seems to have written only when occasion prompted, simply to amuse and occupy himself, subjected to no ruling idea, subordinating himself to no task, conceiving no harmonious whole. In this, as in all else, he became disenchanted, and in the end disgusted. Skepticism induced melancholy, and his correspondence in this connection is most sad. His health failed by degrees, and he wintered regularly at Cannes, sensible that his life was fading away; but he carefully watched over it; the one anxiety that accompanies us to the last breath. By order of his physician he practiced archery, sketched for his amusement the lovely scenery of the neighborhood, and could be met every day in the country walking in silence, with his two English lady friends, one carrying his bow, the other his box of water-colors. So he killed time and learned to be patient. He often went to a lonely cabin, half a league distant, to feed a cat; and caught flies for a lizard which he kept by him; and these were his pets. When the railway brought him a friend, he revived, and his conversation was again brilliant and charming; his letters were always so, his mind and wit the most original and exquisite, remaining unimpaired. But happiness failed him; the future looked dark, nearly as gloomy as it does to us of to-day; and before closing his eyes, he sorrowfully witnessed our national disaster, dying September 23, 1870. In summing up his character and talent, it will be found that, born with an excellent heart, endowed with a superior intellect, having lived an honest man, labored much, and produced several works of the first order, yet he neither utilized his gifts to their utmost extent, nor attained the full happiness to which he might have aspired. Through the fear of being deceived, he was mistrustful in life, in love, in science, and in art, and was himself the dupe of this distrust. One is always so to some degree, and perhaps it is better to resign one's self to it in advance."

The mystery which surrounds these "Letters to an Incognita," their freshness, their epigrammatic brilliancy, their keen and flashing wit, the careless boldness with which they dash off the portraits of the leading men and women of the day, in English as well as in French society, combine to draw attention first of all to them, and they are therefore assigned the first place in this volume. In the translation, special care has been taken to avoid the repetitions which were allowed to disfigure the letters as they were originally published. Everything of general interest has been carefully preserved, so that the letters as they stand reflect with sufficient fullness Mérimée's relations to the Incognita, while they give us as well his pointed comments upon the men and events of his day. This translation of the "Lettres à une Inconnue" is, by the way, the only one through which they have thus far been made accessible to the English reader.

In that section of the volume assigned to Lamartine we have his last published work, "Twenty-five Years of My Life," in Lady Herbert's translation, slightly abridged. The passages which have been exscinded, were mainly digressions or rhapsodies, which any reader of the volume itself would be very likely to omit. The integrity of the narrative itself has been carefully preserved, and all those who have ever felt at all attracted toward Lamartine, will turn to it with an eager interest which cannot fail to be satisfied. "In these Memoirs," as M. de Ronchaud who edits them in the original French, remarks, "his whole nature comes out in its living simplicity. Lamartine's books are full of his genius, but nowhere else has he shown us much of his heart." The second volume of these "Memoirs of Lamartine" is occupied by a translation of the diary of Mme. de Lamartine, "Memoirs of my Mother." These traverse to so great an extent the same ground which is covered by "Twenty-five Years of My Life," that only a few pages have been selected from them for this volume. It is enough to say of "Memoirs of My Mother," in general, that they exhibit Mme. de Lamartine as a deeply spiritual and devout woman, a tenderly affectionate mother, keenly anxious for the welfare of her children, and pardonably proud of the brilliant career of her illustrious son. The distressing circumstances of her death were in painful contrast with the peace and serenity which would seem to have been the more appropriate close of so saintly a life. There are few more affecting passages in any of Lamartine's works than the "Epilogue" in which he describes the heart-rending affliction which overwhelmed him in the death of his mother.

Doubtless George Sand might have given us one of the most notable volumes of reminiscences ever published, had she chosen to do so. Possibly she still holds her material for such a book in reserve. Certainly, her "Reminiscences and Impressions" "(Souvenirs et Impressions") is not by any means the work its title would lead the reader to anticipate. It seems to be a *rechauffé* of articles furnished from time to time possibly to reviews, with scattering personal recollections, few of them so pointed as to possess any general interest. If the share of this volume which is assigned to her may seem disproportionate, the only explanation must be found in the fact that we have here all of her "Reminiscences and Impressions" which is likely to interest the American reader.

LETTERS TO AN INCOGNITA.

PARIS, *Thursday.* — Everything about you is mysterious; and the causes inducing in others a certain line of conduct, impel you always to opposite action. I am becoming accustomed to your ways, and nothing any longer surprises me. Spare me, I beg of you; do not put to too harsh a test the unfortunate habit I have contracted of finding good in all that you do. I was perhaps a little too frank in my last letter, in speaking of my character. An old diplomatist, a shrewd man of the world, has often advised me, "Never say any ill of yourself; your dear friends will say quite enough." Do not, however, take literally my self-depreciation; believe, rather, that my chief virtue is modesty, which I carry to excess, and I tremble lest it injure me in your estimation. I may at another time, when inspired, supply you with an exact catalogue of my qualities; for the list will be long, and being to-day slightly indisposed I dare not project myself into this "progression of the infinite." You cannot guess where I was on Saturday evening, and in what engaged at midnight. I was on the platform of one of the towers of Notre Dame, drinking orangeade and eating ices in the society of four friends and a magnificent moon, with the accompaniment of a great owl flapping his wings. Paris at this hour, and by moonlight, is a superb spectacle, resembling a city of the Thousand and One Nights, the inhabitants of which have been enchanted during their sleep; but Parisians usually go to bed at midnight, and are most stupid in so doing. Our party was a curious one, four nations being represented, each of us with a different way of thinking; but the bore of it was, that some of us, inspired by the moon and the owl, thought it necessary to assume a poetic tone and indulge in platitudes — in fact, little by little every one began to utter nonsense.

I do not know by what chain of ideas this semi-poetic evening leads me to think of one that was not in the least so; a ball given by some young men, to which all the opera dancers were invited. These women are usually very stupid; but I have observed how superior they are in moral delicacy to the men of their class. Only one vice separates them from other women — that of poverty.

PARIS. — Frankness and truth towards women are not desirable — indeed quite the reverse; for see, you regard me as a Sardanapalus because I have been to a ball of *figurantes.* You reproach me as for a crime, and reprove as a still greater crime my praise of these poor girls. Make them rich, I repeat, and only their good qualities will remain; but insurmountable barriers have been raised by the aristocracy between the different classes of society, so that few persons understand how entirely what passes beyond the wall resembles what passes within. I will tell you a story that I heard in this perverse society. In the Rue Saint Honoré lived a poor woman who never left her miserable attic, and who had a little girl twelve years old, neat, reserved, well behaved, who never spoke to any one. Three times a week this child left home in the afternoon, returning alone at midnight, being a supernumerary at the opera. One night she came down to ask for a lighted candle, which being given to her, the porter's wife followed her after a while to the garret, where she found the woman dead on her wretched pallet, and the child occupied in burning a quantity of letters which she drew from a battered trunk. She said, "My mother died to-night, and charged me to burn these papers without reading them." The child knows the name neither of father nor mother, is entirely alone in the world, having no other resource than that of personating monkeys, vultures and devils on the stage. Her mother's last counsel to her was, to remain a *figurante* and to be very good; which she certainly is, even very pious, and does not care to relate her history. Will you be good enough to tell me if there is not infinitely greater merit in this child leading such a life, than belongs to you who enjoy the singular happiness of irreproachable surroundings, and are endowed with a nature so refined as to picture for me, in a measure, the bloom of civilization? I will tell you the truth. I can only endure low society at rare intervals, and through an inexhaustible curiosity respecting all varieties of the human species, seldom entering that of men, there being to me something inexpressibly repulsive in it, especially with us; but in Spain, muleteers and bull-fighters were my friends. I have more than once eaten from the platter of people at whom an Englishman would not look for fear of compromising his self-respect; and I have even drunk from the same leathern bottle with a galley-slave; there was, however, but one bottle, and one must drink when thirsty. Do not believe that I have a predilection for the *canaille.* I simply like to study different manners, different faces, and to hear a different language. Ideas are the same everywhere, and aside from the merely conventional, I do not find good breeding limited to the Faubourg Saint-Germain. All this is Arabic to you, and I know not why I say it. My mother has been very ill, exciting in me great uneasiness, but is now out of danger, and will be in a few days entirely restored to health. I cannot endure anxiety, and during the period of danger I have been in a state of distraction.

As a rule, never select a woman for a confidante; soon or late you would repent of it. Learn also, that there is nothing more common than to do evil for the very pleasure of it. Shake off your ideas of optimism, and be convinced that we are in this world simply to fight against each other. In this connection, I remember that a learned friend who reads hieroglyphics told me that on the Egyptian sarcophagi are often engraved these two words: *life, war;* which proves that I did not originate the maxim just given you. The characters are represented by one of those vases called *canopes*, and a shield with an arm holding a lance.

PARIS. — Your reproaches afford me great pleasure. As to your over-moral relative who says so much evil of me, he recalls Thwackum, who asks: *Can any virtue exist without religion?* Have you read "Tom Jones," a book as immoral as all of mine put together. If it was prohibited, of course you read it. What a droll education you receive in England! And what avails it! Breath is wasted for years in preaching to a young girl, with the certain result that she will desire to know precisely that immoral person for whom it was hoped to inspire her with a holy aversion. What an admirable story is that of the serpent!

All that I know of you pleases me prodigiously. I study you with ardent curiosity. I have certain theories respecting the veriest trifles, — gloves, boots, buckles, to which I attach much importance, having discovered that a certain relation exists between the character of women and the caprice, — or rather, the connection of ideas and the ratiocination, — that dictates the choice of such or such stuffs. I could show, for instance, that a woman who wears blue gowns is a coquette and affects sentiment.

I went the other day on a boating excursion, a number of sailing vessels being on the river, in one of which were several women of a vulgar class. As the vessels reached the shore, from one of them stepped a man about forty years of age who was persistently beating a drum for his own amusement; and while I was admiring the musical organization of this animal a young woman approached him, called him a monster, saying that she had followed him from Paris, and if he declined to admit her to his society he should dearly rue it. The man continued to pound his drum vigorously during this appeal, replying phlegmatically that he would not have her in his boat, whereupon she ran to the vessel moored farthest from the shore and within twenty feet of our own, and sprang into the river, splashing us infamously; but although she had put out my cigar my indignation did not hinder me, aided by my friends, from dragging her out before she had swallowed two glasses of the muddy water. The noble object of such despair had not budged, and grumbled between his teeth: "Why did you pull her out if she wished to drown herself?" Why is it that these cold, indifferent men are the most beloved? I asked myself this question as we sailed home; I ask it still, and I beg you to tell me if you know.

PARIS. — *Mariquita de mi alma* — it is thus I should begin were we at Granada. I believe, notwithstanding my anger, that I love you better in your fits of pouting than I do in any other mood. One sentence of your letter made me laugh like one of the blessed. Without hostile preliminaries for the blow, you tell me *short and sweet:* "My love is promised." You say that you are engaged for life as if it were simply for a quadrille! Very good! My time, it seems, has been profitably employed in discussing love, marriage, and the rest of it! You still say and believe, that when told to "love Monsieur," you at once love. Has your engagement been signed before a notary? When I was a school-boy I received a love-letter with two flaming hearts pierced with a dart, from a seamstress, which precious effusion was captured by the school-master, and I locked up; and, as a denouement of the drama, the object of this budding passion consoled herself with the cruel school-master. Engagements are fatal to the happiness of those who subscribe to them. It is a primal law of nature to hold in aversion whatever savors of the obligatory. All bonds are inherently irksome; and if so trammeled, I seriously believe that you would love *me;* me, to whom you have promised nothing.

To me you appear very devout, superstitious even. This reminds me of a pretty little girl from Granada, who when mounting her mule to cross the Ronda Pass, a route famous for robbers, devoutly kissed her thumb and struck her breast three times, assured by this pious action that the robbers would not dare to show themselves, provided that the *Ingles* — that is myself; with these people all travellers are English — would not swear by the Blessed Virgin and the saints: but only this wicked mode of speech will make these horses move among such roads. See "Tristram Shandy." You are weak and jealous, two qualities not objectionable in a woman, but defects in a man, and I possess them both. Let us cease quarreling and be friends. I kiss the hand that you offer me in pledge of peace.

September. — You allude to special reasons that prevent you from seeking to be with me. I respect secrets, and will not pry into your motives. Some kind busybody may have taken me for the text of a sermon that sways you; nevertheless, in fearing me you would be doing me an infinite wrong. Be reassured I shall never be in love with you; I am now too old and have been too unhappy. I once felt myself falling in love and fled to Spain, one of the finest actions of my life, the cause of the journey never being suspected by the lady. To remain, would have been to commit a great folly — that of offering to a woman in exchange for all that was dear to her, a tenderness that I was conscious of being inadequate to the sacrifice I should have tempted her to make. "Love excuses all, but we must be quite sure that it *is* love;" and this precept, be assured, is more inflexible than those of your Methodistical friends. In me you will acquire a true friend, while I may find a woman with whom I am not in love and in whom I can confide. Should I die this year, you will feel regret at having hardly known me.

The remembrance of your splendid black eyes is no inconsiderable element of my admiration for you. I am old, and nearly insensible to beauty, yet on hearing a fastidious man say that you are very handsome I could not repress a feeling of sadness, and for this reason: that I am horribly jealous (I am not the least in love with you) of my friends, and distressed at the thought that your beauty exposes you to the attentions of men who only appreciate in you that which attracts me the least. The truth is, I am in a frightful humor; nothing makes me so melancholy as a marriage. The Turks who buy a woman after examining her like a fat sheep, are more honest than we who cover our shameful bargain with the transparent varnish of hypocrisy. I have often asked myself what I could say to my wife on my wedding-day, and have found nothing possible unless it be a compliment to her nightcap. The devil would be very cunning to entrap me to such a *fête*. The woman's *rôle* is easier than that of the man. On that day she models herself after the Iphigenia of Racine; but if she observe at all keenly, what droll things she must see! Of course at this *fête* love will be made to you, and you will be regaled with allusions to domestic happiness. When angry, the Andalusians say: "I would stab the sun but for the fear of leaving the world in darkness."

You jest in saying so charmingly that you are afraid of me. You know that I am ugly, capricious in temper, always abstracted, and often tormenting when suffering. Do you not find all this reassuring? You are no pythoness; you will never be in love with me. You are a combination of the angel and the devil, but the latter predominates. You call me a tempter! Dare to say that this word does not apply more strongly to yourself! Have you not thrown a bait to me, poor little fish that I am? And holding me at the end of your line you keep me dancing betwixt heaven and earth, until weary of the sport it may please you to cut me loose, and I shall swim about with the hook in my gills, but never again to find the angler. Adieu, *niña de mi ojos.*

Lady M—— announced to me yesterday that you are going to be married. This being so, burn my letters: I burn yours, and adieu. You know my principle that does not permit me to maintain an intimacy with a married woman whom I have known as demoiselle, with a widow whom I have known as wife. The change in a woman's legal status affects also her various social relations, and always for the worse. In a word, I cannot bear my female friends to marry, therefore, should you marry, let us forget each other. I still love you and commend myself to your prayers.

PARIS. — We are becoming very tender. You say to me: *Amigo de mi alma*, which is very pretty on a woman's lips. It is needless to say that the answer to my question has greatly pleased me. You say, perhaps involuntarily, to my delight, that the husband of a woman who should resemble you would inspire you with true compassion. I believe this readily, and I add that no one would be more unhappy, unless it be the man who should love you. You must be cold and mocking in your fits of ill humor, with an invincible pride that prevents you from saying, "I am in the wrong." Add to this an energy of character causing you to despise complaints and tears. When by the lapse of time and force of events we shall become friends, it will be seen which of the two can more skillfully torment the other. The mere thought of it makes my hair stand on end. Cannot we meet without mystery and as good friends? I am ill and terribly weary. Come to Paris, dear Mariquita, and excite my love anew. I shall never be weary then.

PARIS. — What is your malady? Some heart sorrow? Some mysterious phrases of yours would seem to imply as much. You both suffer and enjoy through the head, but *entre nous*, I do not believe that you are yet in the enjoyment of that viscus (*viscère*) called heart, which is only developed towards twenty-five years of age, in the forty-sixth degree of latitude. Now you are knitting your beautiful black eyebrows and saying: "The insolent fellow, to doubt that I have a heart!" This is, indeed, the great pretension of the day; since the manufacture of such numbers of so-called passionate romances and poems, all women pretend to have a heart. Wait yet a while; when you have a heart in earnest, send me the tidings. You will then regret the happy time in which you only lived by the head, and the ills you now suffer will seem only pin-pricks in comparison with the stabs that will rain upon you with the birth of passion. Your gracious promise to give me your portrait is a double pleasure, as a proof of your increased confidence in me. I am thinking at this moment of the expression of your countenance, which is a little hard: *a lioness, though tame.* I kiss your mysterious feet a thousand times. Adieu.

LONDON, *December.* — Tell me, in the name of God, if you be of God, *querida Mariquita,* why have you not answered my letter? Your last one put me into such a flutter that my reply, on the impulse of the moment, was hardly common sense. Why will you not see me? Your chief motive appears to be the dread of doing something *improper,* as they say here. I do not accept as serious your fear that a more intimate knowledge of me may destroy your illusions. Were this indeed your motive, you would be the first woman, the first human being even, the gratification of whose desires or curiosity had been hindered by a similar consideration. The thing can be *improper* only as regards society. You know in advance that I shall not eat you. Note in passing, that this word *society* makes us unhappy from the moment of donning inconvenient garments at its behests, until the day of our death. A man's discretion, and mine exceptionally, is the greater in proportion that it is trusted. There is, and there will be throughout your life, a conflict between your intuitions and your conventual discipline; thence arises the whole difficulty.

The sea always makes me excessively ill, and *the glad waters of the dark blue sea* are only agreeable to me when seen from the shore; after my first voyage to England it required a fortnight to restore my usual color, that of the pale horse of the Apocalypse. One day at dinner I was seated opposite to Madame V——, who suddenly exclaimed, "Until to-day I thought you were an Indian!"

PARIS, *March,* 1842. — Since you do not refuse my gifts, I send you conserves of rose, bergamot, and jasmine. I offered you Turkish slippers, but have been plundered. Will you have this Turkish mirror in exchange? It may be more acceptable, for you strike me as being even more *coquette* than in the year of grace 1840. It was in December, and you wore ribbed silk stockings.

You are now rich — rich, that is to say free. A capital idea this of your friend, who is another Auld Robin Gray. He must have been in love with you, which you will never confess, for you too dearly love mystery. Why not go to Rome and Naples to see the sun? You are worthy of comprehending Italy, and would return richer in ideas and sensations. I do not advise Greece; your skin is not sufficiently tough to resist all the villainous insects that devour one in that classic land. Speaking of Greece, I send you a blade of grass gathered on the hill of Anthela at Thermopylæ, on the spot where fell the last of the "three hundred." It is not improbable that particles of the dead Leonidas mingle with the constituent atoms of this little flower. It was, I remember, at this very spot, while lying on heaped-up straw and talking to my friend Ampère, that I told him that among the tender memories remaining to me there was only one unmixed with bitterness. I thought of our beautiful youth. *Pray keep my foolish flower.*

I revisited my dear Spain in 1840, passing two months at Madrid where I saw a droll revolution, admirable bull-fights, and the triumphal entry of Espartero, the most comical show possible. I stayed at the country-house of a friend, who in her devotion to me is a sister, and went every morning to Madrid, returning to dine with six charming women, of whom the eldest was thirty-six years old. Owing to the revolution I was the only man permitted to go and come freely, so these six unfortunates had no other *cortejo.* They spoiled me prodigiously. I was not in love with any of them, in which perhaps I was wrong; and though not deceived by these privileges conferred by the revolution, I found it very sweet to be Sultan, even *ad honores.* On my return I indulged in the innocent pleasure of having a book printed, not published, magnificent in binding and engravings. I would offer you this rarity, but it is historic and pedantic, and so bristling with Greek, Latin, and even Osque (do you know in the least what Osque is?), as to be beyond your mark. Last summer, finding myself with money in my pocket, I roved between Malta, Athens, and Constantinople for five months, during which there were not five tedious minutes. I saw the Sultan in varnished boots and a black frock coat, afterwards, covered with diamonds, in the procession of Baïram; on which occasion a very handsome dame, on whose slipper I trod inadvertently, gave me a tremendous blow with her fist, calling me a *giaour*, and this was my sole association with Turkish beauties. At Athens and in Asia I saw the finest monuments in the world, and the loveliest landscapes. The drawback consisted in fleas, and gnats the size of larks. With all this I have grown very old. My firman gives me turtle-dove hair, which is a pretty Oriental metaphor for expressing an ugly truth. Imagine your friend quite gray! Your claim to rival Ionic and Corinthian capitals in my heart, made me laugh. In the first place, I like only the Doric, and there are no capitals, not even those of the Parthenon, which are worth to me the memory of a friendship.

PARIS, *May*, 1842. — If I must be frank, and you know that I cannot correct myself of this defect, I will confess that you struck me as much improved physically, not at all so morally; that you have a very fine complexion, and beautiful hair which I looked at more than your cap, which probably was worthy of admiration, as you seem to be provoked that I did not appreciate it; but I have never been able to distinguish lace from calico. You have still the figure of a sylph, and though rather *blasé* as to black eyes, I never saw finer ones at Constantinople nor at Smyrna.

Now for the reverse of the medal. You have continued a child in many things, and have acquired into the bargain a nice little dash of selfishness and hypocrisy, which may be serviceable, only it is nothing of which one need boast. You do not know how to conceal your first impulses, but think to make amends by a host of puerile evasions. What do you gain by it? Remember Jonathan Swift's fine maxim: *A lie is too good a thing to be wasted.* This magnanimous idea of being hard to yourself, will, assuredly, lead you very far, and a few years hence you will find yourself as happy as the Trappist, who, after having perseveringly scourged himself should one day discover that there is no Paradise. It is your Satanic pride that has hindered you from seeing me. You believe, at least, that you have pride, but it is only a petty vanity well worthy of a devotee. The fashion of the day tends to sermons — do you frequent them? This alone is lacking in you! As respects myself, I am not more of a hypocrite, in which perhaps I am wrong: certain it is that I am not therefore the better liked. Ah! great news! The first Academician out of the forty who shall die will be the cause of my paying thirty-nine visits. I shall pay them as awkwardly as possible, and shall gain thirty-nine enemies. It would be tedious to explain to you this fit of ambition. Suffice it that the Academy is now my blue cachemire. Be happy, but remember this maxim: Never to commit other follies than those agreeable to you. Perhaps you prefer M. de Talleyrand's apothegm, that one must guard against good impulses, because they are nearly always honest.

PARIS, *June*, 1842. — I have received your purse, which exhales a charmingly aristocratic perfume, and if embroidered by yourself does you honor; in it also I recognize your recent taste for the positive. It would have been poetical to value it at one or two stars; and I should prize it even more had you deigned to add to it some lines from your white hands. No, I will not accept your pheasants which you offer in a detestable way, saying, moreover, disagreeable things about my Turkish sweetmeats. It is you who have the palate of a *giaour* in not appreciating the food of houris. Your conscience, I am sure, is often less lenient than I, whom you accuse of hardness and indifference. The hypocrisy that you now cleverly practice, merely as a game, will, in the end, play you a trick — that of becoming a reality. As to coquetry, the inseparable companion of the deplorable vice that you affect, you have long been duly convicted of it, and it became you when tempered by frankness, by heart and imagination. Is it your friendship that you designate as an *essence?* a word I like. Since all that you wish for comes to pass, I humbly pray you to intercede with destiny that I may be an Academician; but the plague must supervene among these gentlemen to favor my chances, to improve which I must also borrow a little of your talent for hypocrisy. I am too old to reform, and in making the effort I should perhaps become even worse than I am. Formerly I had no high opinion of my precious self, but my self-esteem has increased, simply because the world has degenerated. I pass my evenings in re-reading my books which are being republished, and find myself very immoral and sometimes stupid. The question now is to diminish the immorality and stupidity with the least trouble; but at the cost of *blue devils* to myself.

CHALON-SUR-SAONE, *June*, 1842. — Thanks for your prayers, if they are not a mere rhetorical figure. I am aware of your devoutness, which is now the fashion, like blue cachemires. Our French devotion displeases me, being a species of shallow philosophy proceeding from the head and not the heart. When you have seen the Italians you will agree with me that their devotion is alone genuine: only one cannot have it at will, and one must be born beyond the Alps or Pyrenees to possess such faith. You cannot imagine the disgust with which our present society inspires me, and one would say that it had sought by every possible combination to augment the mass of *ennui* apparently necessary in the order of the world; while in Italy everything tends to render existence easy and endurable.

AVIGNON, *July*, 1842. — Since you assume this tone *ma foi*, I yield. Give me brown bread, which is better than none at all, only permit me to say that it *is* brown, and write to me again. You see that I am humble and submissive. The figure of rhetoric of which you believe yourself to be the inventor has been long in use, and might be clothed with an uncouth Greek name, but in French it is known under the less lofty term of lying. Make use of it with me as little as possible, and do not lavish it on others: it must be kept for great occasions. Do not seek to find the world foolish and ridiculous; it is only too much so in reality. It is better to cherish illusions, and I hold several which are perhaps rather transparent, but I exert myself to retain them. I am sorry that you read Homer in Pope, and recommend as preferable Dugas-Montbel's translation, which is the only readable one. If you had the courage to brave ridicule and the time to spare, you would read Planché's Greek Grammar a month to make you sleep, which would not fail of this effect; at the end of two months you would amuse yourself by comparing M. Montbel's translation with the Greek; and two months afterwards you would easily perceive from the ambiguity of phrase, that the Greek has a meaning other than that given by the translator. At the end of a year you would read Homer as you do a melody and the accompaniment; the melody being the Greek, the accompaniment the translation. It is possible that this would incite the wish to study Greek in earnest; but such assiduity is also to presuppose you with neither dresses to occupy you, nor people to whom they may be displayed. Everything in Homer is remarkable. His epithets, so seemingly strange in French, are singularly appropriate. I remember that he calls the sea "purple," and I never understood its application until last year. I was in a little caïque on the Gulf of Lepanto, going to Delphi. The sun was setting, and as it disappeared the sea wore for ten minutes a magnificent tint of dark violet — but this requires the air, the sea, the sun of Greece. I hope that you will never become sufficiently an artist to discover that Homer was a great painter. I hope that you find me this time passably resigned and decorous, *Signora Fornarina!*

PARIS, *August*, 1842. — I congratulate you on your Greek studies, and to begin with something that may interest you, will tell you the word by which in Greek persons possessing like yourself hair of which they are justly proud are described: *efplokamos*. *Ef*, much; *plokamos*, curl. Homer, somewhere says: —

"Nimfi efplokamouça Calypso."
(Curly-tressed nymph Calypso.)

I am sorry that you should set out so late in the season for Italy, which you will see only through atrocious rains that obscure half the charm of the loveliest mountains in the world, and you will be obliged to accept on faith my eulogies on the exquisite skies of Naples. Moreover, you will have no good fruit, but in compensation, *becaficos*, so called because they live on grapes.

While packing my trunk at Avignon, two venerable figures entered, announcing themselves as members of the Municipal Council. I supposed them emissaries from some church, when they informed me with much pomposity and prolixity that they wished to commend to my loyalty and virtue a lady about to travel with me. I replied very crossly that I should be very loyal and virtuous but that I detested travelling with women, whose presence precluded smoking. The mail coach arrived, within which I found a large, handsome woman, simply and coquettishly attired, who declared herself to be always very ill in a carriage, and despaired of reaching Paris alive. Our *tête-à-tête* began, and I was as polite and amiable as I find it possible to be while remaining in a cramped position. My companion talked well, without any Marseillaise accent, was an ardent Bonapartist, very enthusiastic, believed in the immortality of the soul, not too much in the Catechism, and saw things generally *en beau;* nevertheless, I was conscious that she felt a certain fear of me. We were some fifty odd hours alone; but though we chatted immensely I found it impossible to come to any conclusion respecting my neighbor except that she was married, and a person of good society. On arriving at Paris she precipitated herself into the arms of an excessively ugly man, no doubt her father, and raising my hat I was about entering a cab, when my unknown, leaving the gentleman, said in an agitated voice: "Monsieur, I am much moved by the respectful consideration shown me by you, for which I cannot sufficiently express my gratitude; and I shall never forget my good fortune in travelling with so *illustrious* a man."

And this word explains the Municipal Councilors, and the terror of the lady. They had evidently seen my name on the register, and the lady, having read my books, expected to be swallowed alive, which opinion no doubt is shared by many of my feminine readers. This incident put me into a bad humor for two days. It is a singular thing, that having at one period of my life become a very worthless fellow, I lived during two years on my former good reputation; and since resuming my very moral life, I now am considered a scamp. . . . . If you are surprised that the goddesses are blondes, you will be still more astonished at Naples at seeing statues whose hair is painted red. It seems that beautiful women formerly used red, even gold powder; but on the other hand you will see in the pictures of the *Studii*, a number of goddesses with black hair, descriptive of which there is in Greek a terrible word: *mélankhétis:* the χα being a diabolical aspirate.

It distresses me to perceive your rapid progress in Satanism, that you are becoming ironical, sarcastic, and even diabolical, all which words are drawn from the Greek, the meaning of the last being calumniator. You jest at my finest qualities, and even your praise is impaired by a reticence and cautiousness that deprive the commendation of all merit. As for good company, I have often found it mortally tedious. I am vain enough to believe myself not out of place with unpretending persons whom I have long known, and at a Spanish inn with muleteers and Andalusian peasant women. Write that in my funeral oration and you will have told the truth. And if I speak of this, it is that I believe the time approaches for you to prepare it; for I suffer excessively from confused sight, spasms, and frightful headaches, which would indicate some serious affection of the brain, and I may soon become, as Homer says, a guest of gloomy Proserpine. I should be delighted were it to sadden you for a fortnight.

I believe the ancients to have been more amusing than ourselves: they had not such paltry aims, were not preoccupied by such inanities. Julius Cæsar at fifty-three was guilty of follies for Cleopatra, and forgot all for her, nearly to the point of drowning himself actually and figuratively. What statesman of our generation is not callous, completely insensible at the age at which he can aspire to be a Deputy?

The little that I have seen of Greece has enlarged my comprehension of Homer. Throughout the Odyssey one sees the incredible love of the Greeks for their own country. To dwell in a foreign land is to them the greatest of misfortunes; but to die in exile is to them beyond all imagination frightful. You jest at my gastronomy; do you appreciate the entrails so greedily devoured by ancient heroes? They are still eaten, and are truly delicious, being composed of spiced and appetizing little crusts skewered by perfumed mastic wood, which at once explains why the priests reserved for themselves this tempting morsel of the victims.

You ask if there are any Greek novels — there are many, but very tedious in my opinion. "Daphnis and Chloe," translated by Courier is pretentiously *naïf* and not over exemplary. An admirable novel, but very immoral, is "L'Ane de Lucius;" one does not boast, however, of reading it, though a masterpiece. The worst of the Greeks is, that their ideas of morality and decency differ so essentially from our own. If you have the courage to attempt history you will be charmed with Herodotus, who enchants me. Begin with "Anabasis or the Retreat of the Ten Thousand;" take a map of Asia and follow these ten thousand rascals in their journey; it is Froissard *gigantesque.* Lucien is the Greek with the most wit, or rather *our* wit: but he is a libertine and I dare not commend him.

I gratefully appreciate your condescension at the opera in permitting me to look at your face during two hours, and I owe it to truth to say that I admired it greatly, as also your hair, which I had never seen so near. As to your assertion of having refused nothing that I have asked of you, several millions of years in purgatory will be your penance for this fine falsehood. I do not remember comparing you to Cerberus, but you certainly bear him a resemblance, not only in your love for cakes, but in possessing three heads, or rather brains — one of a frightful coquette, the other of an old diplomatist; the third I will not name, as to-day I wish to tell you nothing agreeable. I have returned from seeing "Frédégonde," which was excessively tedious, notwithstanding Mademoiselle Rachel, who has very handsome black eyes without white, as it is said has the devil. You tell me amiably that you do not wish to see me for fear of becoming wearied of me. If I am not mistaken, we have met six or seven times in six years, and adding up the minutes, we may have passed three or four hours together, the half of which was in silence. Admit that it is little flattering to my self-love to be treated thus after an intimacy of six years, and in face of the proofs of regard that you have vouchsafed me ; moreover, pardon the word, I think it somewhat silly. If you believe yourself to be doing wrong in meeting me, do you commit no fault in writing to me? As I am not well versed in your catechism, this remains a perplexing question. I speak harshly perhaps, but you wound me, and I cannot imitate you in ridding myself of a weight on the heart by eating cakes. But I will ask nothing more of you, — for you become every day more imperious, and develop a scandalous refinement in coquetry. You are careful to recall your eyes to me, which I have not forgotten though so seldom seen. You should see me were it only to escape from the atmosphere of flattery surrounding you. When I met you at the house of our friend, your extreme elegance greatly surprised me, and the quantity of cakes necessary to restore you after the fatigue of the opera astonished me still more ; not that I do not place coquetry and *gourmandise* in the first rank of your faults, but I thought the form of these defects a moral one ; believing that you bestowed little thought on your toilette, that you were a woman who eat merely through abstraction, and preferred to make an impression on men by your eyes and clever sayings rather than by your dresses. See how deceived I have been.

December, 1842. — Formerly the absurdities of others amused me, but now I prefer to conceal them from the world. I have also become more humane, and when witnessing lately the bull-fights at Madrid, the pleasurable sensations of ten years previous were not renewed. I have a horror of all suffering, and for some time past have believed in moral suffering. In short, I strive as much as possible to forget my *me;* and this in few words is a list of my perfections. No, I have no *Vanagloria.* I see things too practically, perhaps, having been *escarmentado* through regarding them too poetically. I have passed my life in being praised for qualities that I do not possess, and calumniated for defects that are not mine.

Your letter does not surprise me in the least: for I now know you well enough to be certain that when a good thought strikes you it is at once repented of, and you strive to have it speedily forgotten — but this justice I will do you: that you understand admirably how to gild the most bitter pill. You compare me to the devil. I was quite conscious on Tuesday of not thinking enough about my old books and too much of your gloves and *bottines.* But in spite of all that you say with such diabolical coquetry, I cannot believe that you have the slightest fear of renewing at the Museum our former follies. It pleases you to have some vague mark for your coquetry, and you find it in me; but you do not wish it to be too near, for should you miss the target your vanity would suffer, and perhaps in approaching it closely you would discover it to be not worth your shaft. Have I read you aright?

I suffer terribly and cough incessantly, nevertheless I shall go to hear Rachel declaim tirades from "Phèdre" before several great men, and she will believe my cough to be a cabal against her. This evening I heard Madame Persiani sing, and she has reconciled me to human nature; were I King Saul I should choose her in place of David.

I am told that M. de Pongerville, the Academician, is about to die, which throws me into despair, for I shall not be chosen to replace him, and I wish he could wait until my time shall arrive. He has translated into verse a Latin named Lucretius, who died at the age of forty-three from having taken a philtre to make himself beloved, previous to which he wrote a great poem, atheistic, impious, abominable, on "The Nature of Things." You appear to me to grow more handsome, which I had thought impossible; but one always improves in beauty when in good health; and that comes with a hard heart and good digestion.

December, 1842. — I have been exceedingly ill with my throat, and all the fires of hell in my breast, and have passed several days in bed meditating on the strangeness of this world. I find myself on the declivity of a mountain whose summit, with much fatigue and little pleasure, I have hardly attained, the descent being so steep and tedious that perhaps it would be rather an advantage to fall into a crevice before reaching the bottom; while the only ray of consolation along the whole route has been a little distant sunshine, a few months passed in Italy, Spain, or in Greece while forgetting the whole world, the present, and especially the future. All this is far from gay: but some one brings me four volumes by Doctor Strauss, "The Life of Jesus," which in Germany is called *exegesis*, a pure Greek word they have found by which to express discussion on the point of a needle, but it is very amusing. I have remarked that the more closely a thing is shorn of any useful conclusion, the more amusing it becomes.

There are people who buy furniture of a color to suit their taste, but for fear of spoiling it shroud it in linen covers that are only removed when the furniture is worn out. In all that you do and say, you substitute a factitious for a true sentiment — this perhaps is *decorum*. You say in your letter, "I believe that I have never loved you so well as yesterday" — you should have added, "I love you less to-day." I often repent of being too loyal in my *rôle* of statue. You gave me your soul yesterday: I would have given you mine in return but you did not wish it. Always the linen cover!

Yesterday on returning from a dinner I discovered that I knew by heart the speech of Tecmessa that you admired, and being in a somewhat pensive mood I translated it into English verse, as I abhor French verse.

PARIS, *January*, 1843. — I heartily forgive your jest about the Academy, of which I think less than you believe. Should I ever be an Academician, I shall not be hard as a rock, though perchance a little case-hardened and mummified ; but rather a good fellow at heart.

I am reminded of an incident that occurred a fortnight ago at a dinner given by an Academician for the purpose of presenting Bèranger to Mademoiselle Rachel. A number of celebrities were assembled. Rachel came late and her manner of entering displeased me ; while the men said so many silly things to her, and the women did so many on seeing her, that I remained in my corner ; besides, it is a year since I have spoken to her. After dinner, Bèranger with his candor and usual good sense told her that she was wrong to fritter away her talent in *salons*, there being for her only one true public, that of the Théâtre Français. Rachel appeared to appreciate the advice, and to prove that she benefited by it, at once declaimed the first act of "Esther." Some one was needed to give her the cue, and by her direction a Racine was formally brought to me by an Academician who was officiating as *cicisbeo;* but I replied rudely that I knew nothing about verses and that there were persons present who being in that line would scan them much better. Hugo excused himself on account of his eyes ; another for some other reason, the master of the house being finally victimized. Picture to yourself Rachel costumed in black, standing between the piano and tea-table, with a door behind her, assuming a theatrical pose and expression, the transformation being very fine and vastly amusing. This lasted about two minutes, then she began : —

"Est-ce toi, chère Elise?"

The confidante in the middle of his reply lets fall both book and spectacles, ten minutes passing before he can recover his page and his eyes. The audience perceive that Esther is getting into a rage. She resumes. The door behind opens, a servant enters, who is signed to withdraw. He hurriedly retreats but does not succeed in shutting the door, which remaining ajar swings to and fro, accompanying Rachel with a melodious and most comical creak. This not ceasing, Rachel puts her hand to her heart and grows faint, but, like a person accustomed to die on the stage, giving one time to come to her assistance. During this interlude Hugo and M. Thiers fall to quarreling on the subject of Racine, Hugo asserting that Racine had a narrow mind (*un petit esprit*) and Corneille a master intellect (*un grand*). "You say that," replied Thiers "because you are *un grand esprit;* you are the Corneille" — here Hugo's head assumed an air of great modesty — "of an epoch of which Casimir Delavigne is the Racine." Meanwhile the swoon passes off and the act is finished, but *fiascheggiando.* One of the guests who knows Rachel well, remarked : "How she must have sworn this evening on going away." This is my story ; do not compromise me with the Academicians.

I deeply regret having exposed you through my persistency to such a frightful drenching. It rarely happens to me to sacrifice others to myself, and when it occurs I am filled with all possible remorse. Happiness only gives me strength, while it diminishes yours. *Wer besser liebt?* You laughed at me and received as a jest what I said as to the wish to sleep, or rather the torpor that sometimes steals over one when in a state of happiness so great as to preclude its utterance in words. I observed yesterday that you were under the influence of this sleep, which is worth many vigils, and I was too content to wish to disturb my happiness. It is in exaggerating facts by brooding on them that you have succeeded in making a star-chamber matter of what you have yourself termed *frivolities;* and allow me to say, that the very obstinacy and rabid ferocity with which you thwart me as to these frivolities render them more dear to me, and endue them with a fresh importance. If I must see you only to resist the most innocent temptations, it is the *rôle* of a saint surpassing my strength, and the condition exacted by you that I transform myself into a statue, like the king in the "Arabian Nights, is simply insupportable. The only hypocrisy of which I am capable is that of concealing from those whom I love all the ill they do me; I might sustain the effort for a season; but forever, no. As to our walk, I am like a cat that continues to lick his moustache after lapping milk. Acknowledge that repose, even the *kef*, which is superior to all that is best of this nature, is nothing in comparison with the happiness "that is almost a pain." You claim to have spoiled me, but you do not understand the art; your triumph is to put me in a fury. Adieu, *dearest!*

PARIS, *February*, 1843.—Since seeing you I have been much in society, committing a multitude of academic meannesses which cost me a painful effort, having lost the habit, but doubtless I shall quickly pick it up again. To-day I saw five illustrious poets and writers of prose, and had night not overtaken me the thirty-six visits might possibly have been achieved at a dash. The drollery of it is the meeting one's rivals, several of whom glared as if they wished to eat me alive. Truth to say, I am worn out with this odious drudgery and should be glad to forget it all in an hour with you.

I have been this evening to the Italiens, where, thanks to the *claquers*, my enemy Madame Viardot had a success. I find that I have omitted to attend the Opera House Ball—where, alas! is the happy time in which I so enjoyed it? now it bores me horribly. Do I not seem to you very old? Theodore Hook is dead. Have you read Bulwer's "Ernest Maltravers," and "Alice," which contain charming pictures of old love and young love. You may reflect with pride on the strange influence you have exercised over my ideas and resolutions; you have read my thought as quickly as it was conceived—and yet yesterday, on the strength of a Greek verse, I went to Saint-Germain-l'Auxerrois, full of hope but fruitlessly. Do you remember when we always divined each other's wishes? The other evening at the opera your rainbow costume inspired me with various fancies, but you have no need of coquetry with me. I do not love you better as a rainbow than in black. I have long suspected something diabolical in you, but am somewhat reassured in thinking that I have seen your feet, neither of which is cloven; nevertheless it may be that beneath these *bottines* you have a little claw concealed. I have passed a wretched night of suffering, and as a diversion shall think of your feet and hands.

I have received the sad news of the death by paralysis of poor Sharp,[1] one of my most intimate friends whom I was about to visit in London. I cannot yet accustom myself to the thought of seeing him no more.

My fate will be decided at the Academy on the fourteenth, which corresponds with the ides of March, the day of the death of my hero, Cæsar. Ominous, is it not? Reason encourages me to hope, but a depressing intuition whispers of failure. Meanwhile I conscientiously pay my visits. I find people very polite, quite accustomed to their parts and enacting them very much in earnest, while I strive to play mine with equal gravity, though I find it difficult. Does it not strike you as comical to say to a man, "Monsieur, I believe myself to be one of the forty cleverest men of France; I am worthy of you," and similar facetiæ. This must, moreover, be translated into civil and fitting phrase to suit the various persons; an occupation to weary me beyond endurance if prolonged. I envy the fate of women who have no employment but to make themselves beautiful, and to rehearse the effect to be produced on others. I return your *cravate*, which was found in the anteroom of His Royal Highness the Duke de Nemours, but no one has asked any explanation of its presence in my pocket.

I am full of remorse for my fury, my only excuse being that the transition from our delicious halt in a strange species of oasis, to our walk, was too abrupt — it was falling from heaven to hell. You reproach me with being indifferent to every one; I suppose you simply mean that I am undemonstrative — when untrue to my nature I suffer. Admit also that it is sad, after becoming all that we are to each other, to find you still distrustful of me. Two personalities exist in you: the one all heart and soul; the other a beautiful statue polished by society, draped in silk and cachemire, a charming automaton with most skillfully adjusted springs. We speak to the first, and find only the statue; but why need it be sc

[1] Mr. Sutton Sharp, a very distinguished English barrister.

lovely! You ask if I believe in the soul—nct over much; nevertheless, on reflection I find an argument in favor of the hypothesis, namely: how could two inanimate substances give and receive a sensation by a union that would be simply insipid but for the idea that we associate with it? This is rather a pedantic mode of saying that when two persons who love, embrace each other, they experience a sensation quite different from that communicated by kissing the softest satin. But the argument has its value, and we will discuss metaphysics at our next meeting—a subject of which I am fond, for it is inexhaustible.

You shall have your portrait *en Turquesse*, and I have placed a *narghilé* in your hand to add a local coloring; but I must have my pay, or prepare for a terrible vengeance. I have been asked to-day to contribute a sketch for an album to be sold for the benefit of sufferers by an earthquake, and I shall give them your portrait!

PARIS, *April*, 1843.—You do well not to speak of Catullus. He is not an author to be read during Holy Week, and there are passages in his writings quite impossible to translate into French. We clearly see what love was at Rome towards the year 50 before J. C.; it was, however, a little better than love at Athens in the time of Pericles. Women were already a recognized force: they made men commit follies. Their power arose, not, as is commonly said, through Christianity, but I think through the influence that the barbarians of the North exercised over Roman society. The Germans were capable of exaltation. They loved the soul; the Romans loved little save the body. It is true that for a long period women were without souls: they have none as yet in the East, and it is a pity. You comprehend how two souls speak tó one another, but yours seldom responds to mine. I am glad that you value the verses of Musset, and you are right in comparing him with Catullus, who, however, wrote his native tongue better, while Musset has the defect of not believing more in the soul than Catullus, whom his time excused. Would you believe that a

Roman could say pretty things, and could be tender? I wil. show you some verses that will fit in like wax *à propos* of our usual disputes. You will see that the ancients are worth more than your Wilhelm Meister.

Our walks have become a part of my life, and I hardly understand how I previously existed. In what mood shall I find you? Each time that we meet you are mailed in a fresh panoply of ice that only melts at the end of a quarter of an hour. By the time of my return you will have accumulated a veritable iceberg.

AVALLON, *August*, 1843.—I came here to visit an old uncle whom I have seldom seen. I dislike relations; one is obliged to be familiar with persons whom one has rarely met because they happen to be the son of the same father as one's mother. My uncle, however, is a good fellow, not too provincial, and whom I should find agreeable if we possessed two ideas in common. The women here are as ugly as those of Paris, having, moreover, ankles as thick as posts. In addition to our moral perfections we have the advantage of being the ugliest and most stunted people in Europe. At Vezelay I found myself in a horrible little town perched on a high mountain, bored to death by the country people, and preoccupied by a speech I was to deliver. I am a Representative, and you know me well enough to judge how odious to me is the *rôle* of a public man. While I sketched, a crowd gathered about me, emulating each other in conjectures as to the nature of my occupation. To console me there was an admirable church which owes to me its escape from demolition, and which I first saw soon after meeting you; and I asked myself to-day if we were more mad then than now. There was also a natural terrace that a poet might well call a precipice, where I philosophized on the *me*, on Providence, in the hypothesis that it exists; and finished with the despairing thought that you are far away. I send you an owl's feather that I found in the abbatical church, having read in some book of magic that when a woman places it beneath her pillow she dreams of her friend.

SAINT-LUPICIN, *August*, 1843, 600 *metres above the level of the sea — in the midst of an ocean of very active and famished fleas.* — This village is in the Jura Mountains, is ugly to the last degree, filthy, and populous with fleas. I shall pass a night like those at Ephesus, but at my awaking, unfortunately, I shall find neither laurels nor Greek ruins. There are immense quantities of colossal flowers, a singularly keen and pure air, and the human voice can be heard at a league's distance. I have had leaden skies, a broken wheel, and a poulticed eye, all tolerably remedied : but I cannot become habituated to solitude — solitude in motion, than which there is nothing more sad ; and were I in prison, I should be more at my ease than thus roving alone about the country.

AVIGNON, 1843. — The district that I am now traversing is very fine, but the natives are stupid beyond measure. No one opens his mouth but to praise the country, and this from the priest to the porter. There is no appearance of that tact constituting the gentleman, which I found among the common people of Spain ; but with that exception it is impossible to find a country more nearly resembling Spain. There is the same aspect of town and landscape ; the workmen lie in the shade and drop their cloaks with a tragic air that is Andalusian ; the odor of garlic and oil is mingled with that of oranges and jasmine ; the streets are shaded with linen during the day, and the women have small, well-shod feet ; there is nothing, even to the *patois*, that has not a flavor of Spain. A still closer relation exists in its abundance of gnats, fleas, and other insects, and I have yet two months of this life to pass before seeing human beings !

I have sent my sketches to Paris ; besides, a Roman capital would not interest you, — devils, dragons, and saints forming the decoration. The devils of the first centuries of Christianity are not very seductive, and I am sure that you would not value dragons and saints. I have sketched a Maçon costume for you, the only graceful one I have seen, though the sash is so drolly placed as to afford no advantage in a slender over a thick waist, — the dress would seem to require a special physical organization. The cheapness of cotton stuffs and the facility of communication with Paris have wrought the disappearance of our national costumes. Avignon is filled with churches and palaces, all provided with battlemented and machicolated towers. The palace of the Pope is a model of a fortification for the Middle Ages, which proves what amiable security reigned toward the fourteenth century. There are subterranean chambers used by the Inquisition, with the remains of an infernal complicated machine, and furnaces for heating the irons with which heretics were tortured. The natives are as proud of their Inquisition as the English of their Magna Charta. "We also," say they, "have had *auto-da-fé*, and the Spaniards had none until after us!"

TOULON, *October.* — It is impossible to find a place dirtier or prettier than Marseilles; and these words are especially appropriate to its women. They have expressive countenances, fine black eyes, beautiful teeth, very small feet, and imperceptible ankles; but the pretty feet are shod in thick, cinnamon-colored stockings the color of Marseilles mud, and darned with cotton of twenty different tints. Their dresses are badly made, untidy and covered with stains, while their fine hair owes its lustre mainly to candle-grease. Add to this an atmosphere redolent of garlic mixed with fumes of rancid oil, and you have a picture of the Marseilles beauty. What a pity that nothing can be perfect in this world! Yet, in spite of all, they are ravishing — a positive triumph.

Your letter is admirably diplomatic; you practice the axiom that language has been given to man to conceal his thought; and yet I see between the lines the tenderest things in the world. I think unceasingly of my return to Paris, and my imagination paints I know not how many delicious moments passed at your side.

PARIS, 1843. — *I weary for you*, to make use of an ellipsis that you affect. I did not clearly realize that we were about to part for so long a time. Shall we really see each other no more? We separated without a word, almost without a look. I was sensible of a calm happiness not usual with me, and for a few moments I seemed to wish for nothing more. How ingenious you are in depriving others and yourself of an enchantment that comes so near! Doubtless I am wrong to use the word enchantment, as marmots probably never experience the sensation, and you were one of those pretty animals before Brahma transferred your soul to the body of a woman. But nowithstanding my ill-humor I love better to see you with your grand air of indifference than not at all. The affection you bear me is merely an emanation of the intellect. You are all mind, one of those chilly women of the North who live only through the head. Our characters are as opposite as our *stamina*, and though you may divine my thoughts, you can never comprehend them. Yet, with all these conflicting characteristics a great affinity exists between us; it is Goethe's *Walverwandschaft.* Throw away your faded flowers and come with me to seek fresh ones. You say that sunshine exercises a cheering influence over you,—and for myself, though I love you at all seasons, in all weather, the happiness of seeing you in sunshine is a more exquisite happiness still. Is it possible that you cannot *say* to me all that you write? What is this *bizarre* timidity that hinders frankness, prompts you to wrap your thoughts in words more perplexing than the Apocalypse, and to assert the most extraordinary falsehood rather than allow a word of truth to escape which would giye me such pleasure? Do you believe in the devil? In my opinion the pith of the matter lies there. If he terrifies you, contrive that he do not carry you off. I do not guaranty my catechism, which, however, I believe to be the best. I have never sought to make converts, but, up to the present time, neither has my conversion been accomplished by others.

Yesterday evening I went to the opera, where they proposed to close the doors, Ronconi being drunk or in prison for debt; but yielding to our clamor they gave us "L'Elisir d'Amore;" after which I corrected proofs until three o'clock in the morning. I do not concern myself so much about the Academy as you suppose. I have hardly a chance of success. Do you know any magic that will conjure my name from the deal-box called Urn?

PARIS, *March*, 1844.[1] — Many thanks for your congratulations, but I wish for something better; to see and walk with you. I think you take the matter too tragically. Why do you weep? The "forty chairs" were not worth one little tear. I am very heartily gratified, the more that I expected defeat; and my mother who was suffering from acute rheumatism was suddenly cured. I am worn out, demoralized, and completely "out of my wits." Then my novel, "Arsène Guillot," makes a signal *fiasco* and rouses the indignation of all the self-styled virtuous people, especially the women of fashion who dance the polka and throng to the sermons of Père Ravignan, and who go so far as to liken me to a monkey who climbs to the top of the tree and makes grimaces at the world below. I believe that some votes have been lost by this scandal; on the other hand, some have been gained. Now, to show my greatness of soul, I must rush about thanking friends and enemies. I had the good fortune to be blackballed seven times by persons whom I detest, yet who tell me that they were my warmest partisans; but it is a happiness not to be burdened with gratitude towards those whom we hold in slight esteem. My Homer deceived me, or rather it was M. Vatout to whom the threatening vaticination was addressed.

March, 1844. — I fear that the address may have seemed too long. I am still shivering from the cold, and you may have perceived my terrible cough, which might have been mistaken for a cabal. Did you prefer the full dress to the frock coat? I had some difficulty in discovering you hidden beneath your neighbor's bonnet — another bit of childishness. Did you see what I sent you, in full view of the Academy? But of course you never wish to see anything. Why will you dispute on

[1] His election to the French Academy.

this text: "Which loves the best?" A desirable preliminary would be to come to an agreement as to the meaning of the verb, and this we shall never do; we are both too ignorant, and above all too ignorant of each other. More than once I have fancied you to be clearly revealed, but you always escape me. I was right in calling you Cerberus, "three gentlemen in one." Our mutual concessions only result in making us more unhappy; and, more clear-sighted than you, I greatly blame myself, for I have made you suffer in prolonging an illusion that I should never have conceived. For you I have no reproaches. You wished to reconcile two incompatible things, but in vain. Should I not be grateful that you essayed the impossible for my sake? On the whole, perhaps you will one day come to regard our folly only in its fairest light, will remember only the happy moments we have passed together.

Consider if it be not sad for me to find myself always in conflict with your pride, my great enemy, or rather rival in your heart, and which triumphs over your tenderness, in comparison with which it is a Colossus to a pigmy. This premeditated pleasure, or, I prefer to believe, instinct that leads you to excite in me a desire for what you obstinately refuse, is in reality a species of selfishness. All that wounds your pride stirs you to rebellion; and unconsciously this colors the most trivial details. You are happy, you tell me, when I kiss your hand, and you yield yourself to the feeling because your pride is satisfied by this demonstration of humility. You wish me to be a statue that you may be my life, my soul-awakener; but you wish for no reciprocity in the happiness to which I aspire, as that would imply an equality that displeases you. I shall never place my pride and happiness in the same scale, therefore if you will kindly suggest new formulas of humility, I will adopt them without hesitation. Is not the friendship which so strangely unites us, a sweeter, more living force than all the victories gained by your demon pride?

Paris, 1844.—It is decided that I go to Algeria next month; and while you are learning Greek I am studying

Arabic, a diabolical language of which I shall never acquire two words. I passed a day at Strasbourg, exhorting the authorities with sublime eloquence to restore an ancient church ; their reply being that they were in greater need of tobacco than monuments, and that they should convert the church into a storehouse. The cathedral that formerly I liked so much appears absolutely ugly, and even the wise and foolish virgins of Steinbach hardly found grace in my eyes. You are right in liking Paris so well ; it is, after all, the only city in which one can truly live.

I dined yesterday with General Narvaez — an entertainment in honor of his wife's birthday. Few ladies except Spanish were present. One was pointed out to me who is starving herself to death through love, and is gently fading away. This species of suicide must seem very cruel to you. There was another demoiselle, whom General Serrano has deserted for her fat Catholic Majesty ; but she is not dying of it, and seems even to be in excellent health. There was also Madame Gonzalez Bravo, sister of the actor Romea, and sister-in-law of the same Majesty, who, it is said, gives herself a large number of sisters-in-law. This one is very pretty and very clever.

PARIS, 1844. — We separated yesterday mutually discontented, and both were in the wrong. It is evident that we can no longer meet without quarreling horribly. We both desire the impossible. You — that I should be a statue ; I — that you should cease to be one. Every fresh proof of this impossibility, which at heart we have never doubted, is cruel for both. For my part I regret all the pain I have caused you. I too often give way to impulses of absurd anger ; it would be as reasonable to feel angry against ice for being cold. I hope that you will forgive me ; no resentment remains, only a heavy sadness. Adieu, since only at a distance can we be friends. When both shall be old, we may perhaps meet again with pleasure ; meanwhile, in misfortune or in happiness, remember me. Once more, while I have the courage, adieu.

Paris, 1844. — My occupation at this moment is tedious and low beyond measure; I am soliciting votes for the Academy of Inscriptions. The most absurd scenes occur, and I am often seized with a wish to laugh, which must be repressed for fear of shocking the gravity of the Academicians. I embarked somewhat blindly in the affair, but my chances are not bad. You are wrong to be jealous of Inscriptions. I have a little *amour propre* in the matter; just as in a game of chess with a skillful adversary, but neither loss nor gain will affect me a quarter so much as one of our quarrels. But what a vile calling is this of solicitor! Did you ever see dogs enter the hole of a badger? When experienced in the game they have an appalled look on entering, and often come out more quickly than they go in, for it is an ugly brute to visit, is the badger. I always think of the badger when about to ring the bell of an Academician, and "in the mind's eye" I see myself an exact likeness of that dog. However, I have not yet been bitten.

Poitiers, 1844. — No doubt you have amused yourself exceedingly, which I cannot but believe to be synonymous with an indulgence in coquetry. Since leaving Paris my life has been unspeakably disagreeable. Like Ulysses, I have seen much of manners, men, and cities, and find them all very ugly. I have had several attacks of fever that astonished and grieved me as proving that I am growing old. I find the country the flattest and most insignificant in France, but fine forests, great trees, and vast solitudes abound, wherein I should like to meet you. I pass my time in meditating on our walks. I applaud Scribe for having made a virtuous and neo-catholic public laugh with the prizes for virtue; and I am equally surprised as to what you say of his elocution, as formerly he read abominably. It must be the academic robe that bestows this self-command; and this restored a little hope to me.

Perpignan, 1844. — I have been tormented by an absurd idea which I hardly dare to tell you. While visiting the arena of Nîmes with the architect of the department, who was explaining some repairs under his direction, I observed ten paces from me a charming bird a little larger than a titmouse, gray body, with white, red, and black wings, which, perching itself on a cornice, looked fixedly at me. The architect, a great sportsman, had never seen one resembling it. As I approached it flew off, poising itself again a few steps distant, still regarding me closely; and wherever I went, in every story of the amphitheatre, it followed me, its flight being noiseless, like that of a night bird. The next day the scene was repeated. I brought bread, it would not touch it; I then threw it a grasshopper, which it equally disregarded, still watching me. The most learned ornithologist of the town tells me that no bird of this species exists in this region. Finally, at my last visit to the amphitheatre, my bird still followed my steps so far as to enter a dark and narrow corridor where a day bird would seldom venture. I then remembered that the Duchess of Buckingham saw her husband under the form of a bird the day of his assassination, and the idea flashed upon me that you were dead and had assumed this shape to visit me. In spite of myself this nonsense distressed me, and I was enchanted to find your letter dated the day on which I first saw my marvelous bird.

A fair is in progress here, and the town additionally thronged with Spaniards flying from the epidemic, so that I was unable to obtain lodging at an inn, and should have been reduced to a bed in the street but for the commiseration of a hatter. I write in a cold little room with a smoking chimney, cursing the rain that dashes against my window; the woman who serves me speaks Catalan, and only understands me when I speak Spanish; while, worst of all, the flood threatens to carry away the bridge and detain me here, a wretched prisoner. An admirable situation for the expression of ideas.

I have been to the Fountain of Vaucluse, where I wished to inscribe your name, but there were so many atrocious verses, so many Sophies and Carolines, that I would not profane it by such bad company. Parthenay I found a horrible town of *chouans*, with an abominable tavern where they made an infernal noise, and mixed so much stable with my dinner as to make it impossible for me to eat. At Saint-Maixent I saw women with headgear of the fourteenth century, and the waist of the dress of nearly the same period, allowing the chemise to be seen, which is of coarse house-cloth, buttoned under the chin, and open like men's shirts ; and in spite of the ginger-bread beneath I thought it very pretty.

PARIS, *February*, 1845. — Everything passed off better than I had hoped.[1] I was perfectly self-possessed, and am well content with the public, though I know not if it be so with me. All is well since you did not find me ridiculous. I should have lost my confidence had I known you to be present, in view especially of my tarragon-colored coat, and my face *idem*.

TOULOUSE. — Fortunately I find here your letter, for I was furious at your silence. You are never so near forgetting me as when persuading me that I am in your thought. You ask me to pet you, but I am in too bad a humor, having been in a continuous rage this past fortnight against you, against myself, the weather, and the architects. I passed four-and-twenty hours at the house of a Deputy and if I were ambitious of being a politician this visit would have completely quenched my aspirations. What a calling ! what people one must see, conciliate, flatter ! I say with Hotspur : "I had rather be a kitten and cry mew." Slavery for slavery, I prefer the court of a despot ; at least the greater part of despots wash their hands. In England, no doubt, Lady M—— will beset you again with her fine theories "about the baseness of being in love." God knows if you will not return three quarters English. While you are luxuriating in melting peaches, I am eating yellow, acid ones of a singular but not unpleasant flavor, and figs of every color. I am immeasurably bored in the evening, and begin to wish for the society of bipeds of my own species. I count the provincials as naught, being fatiguing to my eyes and entirely foreign to my circle of thought.

[1] His reception at the French Academy.

BARCELONA, 1845. — I have reached the goal of my long journey, and have been admirably received by my archivist, who had already prepared my tables and the ancient books in which I shall lose what remains of my sight. To find his *despacho*, a gothic hall of the fourteenth century must be traversed, and a marble court planted with orange-trees as tall as our lime-trees, and covered with ripe fruit. This is very poetical, and as regards comfort and luxury recalls, as does my chamber, the Asiatic caravanserai. However, it is better than Andalusia, though the natives are inferior and have a fatal defect in my eyes, or rather ears, in that I understand nothing of their gibberish. At Perpignan, I met two gypsies who were cropping mules, and I spoke *caló* to them to the great horror of my companion, a colonel of artillery; while they, finding me even more skilled than themselves in the *patois*, offered a striking testimony to my attainments of which I was not a little proud. In summing up the results of my journey, my conviction is, that it was unnecessary to come so far, and that my history could have been satisfactorily accomplished without disturbing the venerable dust of Aragonese archives.

MADRID, *November*, 1845. — I have been installed here a week in the midst of intense cold, rain, and a climate quite similar to that of Paris; only, I look on snow-capped mountains and live familiarly with very fine Velasquez. Thanks to the ineffable slowness of these people, I have only to-day begun to ferret among the manuscripts, as an academic council was necessary to permit me to examine them, and I know not how many intrigues to enable me to obtain information as to their existence.

I find this country much changed, and less agreeable since my last visit. Persons whom I left friends are now mortal enemies; many of my former acquaintances have become grandees, and very insolent. Every one thinks aloud, with but slight consideration for others, and a frankness prevails that amazes us Frenchmen, and me the more, inasmuch as you have lately accustomed me to something very different. You should make a tour beyond the Pyrenées to take a lesson in frankness. You can form no conception of the expression of the swain's face when the beloved object does not arrive at the appointed hour, nor of the noise of the escaping sighs; but such scenes are so common as to create no scandal nor tittle-tattle. I see happy lovers, and find that they take advantage of the confidence and intimacy accorded by their *innamoratas.* The most romantic do not comprehend in the least what we term gallantry: the lovers here, truth to say, are merely husbands non-authorized by the church. They are the *souffre douleur* of the legal husband, execute commissions and nurse Madame when she takes medicine. Notwithstanding your infernal coquetry, and your aversion for the truth, I love you far more than all these over-frank people. Do not take advantage of this avowal. It is so cold that we shall have no bull-fight; but a number of balls are announced, the tedium of which is inexpressible.

August, 1846, *on board a steamboat.* — I have been among the mountains seeking some spot remote from electors and candidates, but I found such quantities of flies and fleas that I am not sure if the elections be not preferable. Yesterday evening I spent with peasant men and women, making their hair stand on end with ghost stories. There was a magnificent moon that lighted up their regular features and showed the fine black eyes of these damsels, while idealizing the condition of their hands and stockings. I went to bed very proud of my success with this, to me, novel audience; but in the morning on seeing my *Ardéchoises* by sunlight, *con villanos manos y pies,* I almost regretted my eloquence.

PARIS, 1846. — I find the provinces more stupid and unendurable each year. I could not well describe the tedium and various annoyances of this little tour. It recalls Clarence's dream: —

"I would not spend another such a night,
Though 't were to buy a world of happy days."

Paris is absolutely empty of intelligent inhabitants, only cap-makers and Deputies remaining, which is nearly the same thing. I am even more isolated here than usual, depressed by something of the feeling of an *emigré* who on returning to his country finds a new generation. It will strike you that I have grown horribly old — all of which simply means that I am sad, very cross, and that it is you, our walks, which I need. Perhaps when the sea air shall have tarnished your dresses, or fresh ones arrive from Paris, you will send me a thought. There is nothing on earth half so charming to a woman, it is said, as to display pretty toilettes. I can offer you no equivalent for these joys; but I should suffer too much in believing you to be so constituted. I learn, with pleasure, that you are so heartily wearied at ——, which I predicted. After living in Paris, the provinces are insupportable; one says and does numberless enormities that are overlooked in Paris, but which in a village are magnified to the size of a house.

BONN, 1846. — When once launched on a journey I have the utmost difficulty in coming to a halt; and very seductive promises will be needed to prevent me from pushing on to Lapland. I have been six days in this admirable country, I mean Rhenish Prussia, where civilization is very advanced, with the exception of the beds, which are still four feet long, the sheets three. I lead an altogether German life. I rise at five o'clock and go to bed at nine, after partaking of four meals, which routine suits me quite well; and I am not yet ill with doing nothing save opening my mouth and eyes. Only, the German women have become horribly ugly since my last visit.

With respect to monuments, I am by no means satisfied with those I have seen, the German architects appearing to me even worse than our own. They have denuded the Minster at Bonn, and painted the Abbey at Lahr in a way to make one grind one's teeth. The scenery of the Moselle is very much overpraised, and I have seen nothing really striking since passing the Tmolus. My admiration is exclusively reserved for the umbrageous foliage and for their fine conception of the *cuisine;* here the most important occupation is *zu speisen.* All honest people after dining at one o'clock take tea and cakes at four, go to a garden at six to eat a roll and stuffed tongue, which enables them to sustain nature until eight, when they go to a hotel to have their supper. What becomes of the women during this period I do not know, but it is certain that from eight to ten o'clock not a man remains in the house, each one being at his favorite hotel, eating, drinking, and smoking; and the reason of this may, I think, be found in the large feet of these ladies and the excellence of Rhenish wine.

PARIS, *March*, 1848. — I have never been more sadly shocked by the stupidity of the Northern people, and also by their inferiority to those of the South, than during my recent tour, the average native of Picardy striking me as much below the lowest class of Provence; in addition to which I nearly perished with cold in all the inns to which my evil destiny led me.

I am tormented by the failure of the —— firm, in which I fear your interests also are at stake; and each day will bring us fresh disturbance. We must sustain each other and share the little courage remaining to us. You are too much alarmed; but it is difficult to give advice and to see clearly through the fog that stretches over our future. Many persons believe Paris, all things considered, to be safer than the country, and I am also of this opinion. I have no fear of a street battle, first, because no sufficient motive exists; then that strength and audacity are on the one side, while I see only dullness and cowardice on the other. If civil war should break out, it will be first declared in the country, as great irritation has been aroused against the dictatorship of the capital, and perhaps measures, now impossible to foresee, may lead to this result in the West. As to the consequence of the riots, contrast those of the first revolution in Paris with the one two years ago at Buzançais, — more deplorable than all those of '93. Everything passed off quietly yesterday, and we shall have numerous similar processions before any shot will be fired, if indeed that should ever happen in this timid country.

PARIS, *May*, 1848. — All has passed off well, for the reason that they are such fools that the Chamber, notwithstanding all its faults, has proved to be stronger than they. There are neither killed nor wounded, everything is quiet, and an excellent feeling prevails between the people and the National Guard. The leading insurgents have been arrested, and so many troops are under arms that for some time to come there will be nothing to fear. I have witnessed some highly dramatic scenes. I am worn out with a night's service with the Guards, but, after all, fatigue has its advantage at this time. The happiness of seeing you is as great under the Republic as under the Monarchy, and you must not be avaricious in its bestowal. But the most important, pressing thing to tell you is, that each day I love you more and more, and I should be glad could you summon courage to say the same to me.

June, 1848. — I returned this morning from a little campaign of four days, during which I ran no danger and was enabled to see the horrors of the day and of this country. In the midst of my distress I grieve above all for the folly of France: it is unequaled. I cannot see that it will ever be possible to turn her aside from the savage barbarism in which she shows so strong an inclination to wallow. I hope that your brother is safe: I do not think that his legion was seriously in action. I will hastily relate a curious incident or two before going to bed. The La Force prison was protected for several hours by the National Guard and surrounded by the insurgents, who said to the soldiers: "Do not fire on us and we will not fire on you — take care of the prisoners." To watch the battle I entered a house that had just been rescued from the rebels, and asked the occupants, "Did they take much from you?" "They stole nothing." Add to this, that I led a woman to the abbey who had employed herself in cutting off the heads of the Guards with her kitchen knife; and that I saw a man whose two arms were red with the blood of a dying soldier whose belly he had ripped up, laving his hands in the gaping wound. Do you begin to understand somewhat of this great nation? What is quite certain is, that we are going headlong to the devil.

July, 1848. — Paris is, and will be quiet for some time to come. I do not think that the civil, or rather the social war is at an end, but another battle so frightful as the recent one seems impossible, the recurrence of the infinity of circumstances necessary to bring it about not being probable. Of its hideous results which your imagination doubtless paints, you will find but few traces, the glazier and house-painter having already effected their removal ; but you will see many long faces. What can one do ? the *régime* is *de facto*, and we must accustom ourselves to it. By and by we shall cease to think of the morrow, and on awaking in the morning shall be happy in the certainty of an undisturbed evening. The days are long and warm, and as tranquil as could be wished, or rather hoped for under the Republic. All the signs foretell a prolonged truce. The disarming is effected with vigor, and produces good results. One curious symptom is remarked ; namely, that in the insurgent faubourgs any number of informers can be found to point out the hiding-places and even the leaders of the barricades. It is a good sign, you know, when wolves fall to fighting among themselves. The 14th of July passed by very quietly, notwithstanding the sinister predictions with which we were favored. The truth — if it can be discovered under the government under which we have the good fortune to live — the truth is, that our chances for tranquillity have been singularly increased. To bring about the events of June, several years of organization and four months of arming were requisite. A second representation of this bloody tragedy appears to me impossible ; nevertheless, some little plot, several assassinations, and a few riots are still probable. We shall have perhaps a half century in which to perfect ourselves, the one party in the construction of barricades, the other in their destruction. Paris is now being filled with mortars and howitzers, both transportable and efficacious — a novel argument, and said to be excellent.

I went yesterday to Saint-Germain to order a dinner for the Society of Bibliophiles, where I found a cook not only capable, but eloquent, who comprehended at once the most fantastic dishes that I proposed. This great man resides in the portion of the palace in which Henry IV. was born, which commands one of the loveliest views in the world, while a few steps bring one to a wood with great trees and magnificent undergrowth. And not a soul to enjoy all this !

You resemble Anteus, who renewed his strength in touching the earth. *You* no sooner touch your native soil than you relapse into your old defects. Your letter does not tell me how long I am to suffer the purgatory of your absence. It was redolent of a perfume so much the more delicious from being familiar to me, and which brings to me so many charming associations. I think of you unceasingly ; even while looking at the fighting at the Bastille my thoughts were of you.

August, 1848. — This evening while my friend M. Mignet was strolling with Mademoiselle Dosne in the little garden fronting the residence of M. Thiers, a ball came down without the least noise, struck the house very near Madame Thiers's window and glancing thence wounded a little girl seated beyond the garden railing. The ball was quickly extracted, and no ill will ensue save a slight scar : but for whom was it intended ? Mignet ? that is impossible. Mademoiselle Dosne ? still more so. Neither Madame nor M. Thiers was at home. No one heard the explosion, the ball was of regulation size, and air-guns are of a much smaller calibre. I believe it to have been a republican attempt at intimidation, as foolish as all else that is done in this our day. Cavaignac says : "They will kill me, Lamoricière will succeed me, then Bedeau ; after whom will come the Duc d'Isly, who will sweep everything clean." Does this not strike you as prophetic ? No one believes in an intervention in Italy. The Republic will be even rather more cowardly than the Monarchy ; they may, however, make a pretence of allowing it to be supposed that intervention is probable, hoping by this ruse to obtain a congress, protocols, and a compromise. One of my friends, just returned from Italy, was plundered by the Roman volunteers, who find that travellers are made of better stuff than the Croats. He asserts that it is impossible to make the Italians fight, with the exception of the Piedmontese. Throw aside your Romaic; it will be love's labor lost. In vainly trying to learn it I forgot my Greek, and it will play you the same trick. I am surprised at your facile comprehension of this gibberish, which as a language, moreover, will soon disappear, for Greek is already spoken at Athens, and Romaic will only be used by the lower orders. Since 1841, not a single Turkish word, formerly so frequent, has been heard in the Greece of King Otho.

Yesterday, at the general competition for prizes, one was awarded to an urchin named *Leroy*, whereupon his comrades exclaimed "*Vive le roi!*"

General Cavaignac who assisted at the ceremony laughed with a very good grace: but the same boy receiving yet another prize, the applause became so uproarious that the general lost countenance and twisted his beard as if he would pluck it out by the roots.

August, 1848. — We hear rumors of fresh riots; and now the cholera is coming to complicate matters. M. Ledru is thought to be inciting a disturbance by way of protest against the administrative inquiry. The situation closely resembles that of Rome during Catiline's conspiracy, only there is no Cicero. A most grievous symptom is, that Citizen Proudhon has a great number of adherents, his little sheets being sold in the faubourgs by thousands — all of which is sad, but to me the *ennui* of the approaching rain and cold is more serious and much more certain than the riot. I suffer much, and should be excessively vexed to die before our breakfast at Saint-Germain.

LONDON, *June*, 1850. — The most decided impression received from this journey is that the English are individually stupid (*bêtes*), but an admirable people *en masse*. Everything that can be done by the aid of money, good sense, and patience, they do; but of the arts they have no more notion than my cat.

The Nepaulese princes are here, with whom you would fall in love. They wear flat turbans bordered with enormous pear-shaped emeralds, and are a mass of satin, cachemire, and gold. They are of a deep milk and coffee color, have a good air, and appear to be intelligent.

We are going to Hampton Court to avoid the chances fc suicide that the *Lord's Day* in this city would not fail to offe1 I dined yesterday with a bishop and a dean, who have made me even still more a socialist. The bishop belongs to what the Germans call the rationalist school ; he does not even believe what he preaches, and on the strength of his black silk apron enjoys five or six thousand pounds a year and passes his time in reading Greek. The women all look as if made of wax ; and wear such expansive bustles that the pavement of Regent Street is only wide enough to hold one woman at a time. I passed yesterday morning in the new House of Commons, which is a frightful monstrosity ; I had previously no conception of what could be accomplished with an utter want of taste and two millions sterling. I have strong fears of becoming a thorough socialist by dint of eating admirable dinners from silver gilt plates, and seeing persons who win forty thousand pounds sterling at the Epsom races. There is as yet no probability of a revolutionary outbreak here. The servility of the lower orders, of which we see each day some fresh example, conflicts with our democratic ideas : it is a question of moment to know if they are more happy.

SALISBURY, *June*, 1850. — I begin to have enough of this region. I am worn out with the perpendicular architecture, and the manners, equally perpendicular, of the natives. I have passed two days at Cambridge and Oxford with the reverends, and, all things considered, I prefer the Capuchins. I am especially furious against Oxford. A Fellow had the insolence to invite me to dinner. There was a fish four inches long, in a great silver dish, and a lamb cutlet in another : all this served in magnificent style, with potatoes in a dish of carved wood. But never was I so hungry. This is the result of the hypocrisy of these people. They like to show their abstinence to foreigners, and, eating luncheon, they do not dine. Were it not broad day at eight o'clock in the evening, one might believe it to be December, which does not hinder the women from going out with open parasol. It is impossible to see anything more ridiculous than an Englishwoman in the hoop that is worn here.

I have just committed a blunder. I gave half a crown to a man in black who showed me over the cathedral, and then I asked him for the address of a gentleman for whom I had a letter from the dean. He proved to be the very person to whom the letter was addressed. He looked very foolish, and so did I: but he kept the money.

Who is a Miss Jewsbury, rather red-haired, who writes novels? I met her recently and she told me that she had dreamed all her life of a pleasure that she believed impossible, that of seeing me — *verbatim*. She has written a novel entitled "Zoe." Will you, who read so much, tell me who is this person for whom I am a romance.

PARIS, *June*, 1851. — Yesterday I accepted an invitation from the Princess Mathilde to see the Spanish dancers, who are very *médiocre*. The dance at the Mabille has killed the *bolero*, and these dames wore such a quantity of crinoline as to prove clearly the encroachment of civilization. A girl and her old duenna amused me by their intense surprise at finding themselves beyond the *tierra* of Jesus; they were as perfect barbarians as could be desired.

PARIS, *December*, 1851. — The last battle, I believe, is now being fought; but who will win? Should the President lose, it seems to me that the heroic Deputies should give way to Ledru-Rollin. I have returned home horribly fatigued, and have met none but madmen. The look of Paris recalls that of February, except that now the soldiers are very fierce and terrify the citizens. The military are sure of success, but we understand their almanac. However this may be, we have just escaped a reef and are sailing towards the unknown.

PARIS, 1852. — I am threatened with a lawsuit for contempt of court and attack upon the final judgment; while the School of Charts is also sharpening its claws to tear me to pieces. I shall be compelled to undergo an examination and to engage in desperate polemics. In case I fail, try to keep well and come to see me in prison. I do not know whether they will hang me, but I am very *fidgetty* at the thought of a public ceremony in presence of the very cream of the rabble, and three imbeciles in black gowns as stiff as pickets and convinced of their own importance, to whom one cannot dream of expressing one's contempt for their gowns, their person, and their mind.

May, 1852. — Four days in prison and a thousand francs fine! My lawyer argued well, the judges were civil, and I not at all nervous. I shall not appeal. I pass my time in reading Beyle's correspondence. It has rejuvenated me twenty years. It is as if I were making the autopsy of the thoughts of a man whom I have known intimately and whose ideas respecting men and things had grown singularly colorless by the side of my experience. This renders me sad and gay twenty times within the hour, and makes me regret having burned Beyle's letters to me.

CARABANCHEL, 1853. — On arriving here I found preparations for a *fête* at which a comedy was to be played and a *loa* (a dithyrambic dialogue) recited in honor of the lady of the house and her daughter. My services were called into requisition to paint skies, repair decorations, and design costumes, not to enumerate the rehearsals of five mythological goddesses, who on the fatal day looked exceedingly pretty but were overcome with terror. The audience applauded warmly, without understanding in the least the nonsensical rigmarole of the poet author of the *loa*. The comedy was better, and I admire the facility with which the young girls of society transform themselves into passable actresses. During supper a *protégé* of the Countess improvised some pretty verses that moved the heroine to tears and disposed every one else to drink rather too generously. As there are nine ladies here without a gentleman, I am called at Madrid, "Apollo." Of the nine Muses five unfortunately are mothers, but the remaining four are true born Andalusians with little ferocious airs that are ravishing, especially when in their Olympian costume with peplum, which through love of euphony they persist in calling *peplo.*

MADRID, *October*, 1853.—I went yesterday to see Cucharès, the best matador since Montès. The bulls were so indifferent that it was necessary to excite them by little fiery darts. Two men were thrown into the air, and for a moment we thought them dead, which imparted some slight interest to the spectacle; otherwise everything was detestable. The bulls no longer have any spirit, and the men are not much better than the bulls. The ugly convent of the Escurial is as sad as when I saw it twenty years ago, but civilization has penetrated its walls and one finds iron bedsteads and cutlets, but no longer fleas and monks. The absence of the latter distinctive element renders Herrera's heavy architecture still more ridiculous.

I will bring you the garters, which I had dfficulty in finding. Civilization makes such rapid progress that on nearly every leg the *elastic* has replaced the classic *ligas* of former days; and when I asked the chamber-maids to show me a shop where they were sold they indignantly crossed themselves, saying that they no longer wore such obsolete fashions, which were only in use by the common people. Mantillas are nearly as rare; they are superseded by bonnets; and such bonnets!

Last week the *fête* of *Saint Eugénie* was celebrated at the French embassy by a ball, at which Madame ——, wife of the United States Minister, appeared in a costume so designed as to make one split with laughter—black velvet bordered with gold lace and tinsel, and a tawdry diadem. Her son, who looks like a boor, made inquiries respecting the position of the persons present, and having obtained satisfactory information sent a challenge to a very noble, very rich duke, a great simpleton, and desirous of living yet a long time. The parley still continues, but no one will be killed.

I am re-reading "Wilhelm Meister," a strange book, in which the finest possible things alternate with the most absurd childishness. In all that Goethe wrote there is a singular mingling of genius and German silliness (*niaiserie*): was he laughing at others or at himself? On my return remind me to give you "The Elective Affinities," the oddest, most anti-French of all his works. No one reads at Madrid. I have asked myself how the women pass their time when not making love, and I find no plausible reply. They are all thinking of being empresses. A demoiselle of Granada was at the play when it was announced in her box that the Countess de Teba was to marry the Emperor. She rose with impetuosity, exclaiming: "*En ese pueblo no hay parvenir.*"[1]

The absorbing question here is, whether the Ministry will remain in, or whether there will be a *coup d'état*. The house in which I reside is neutral ground, where the Ministers and leaders of the Opposition meet, which is agreeable for lovers of news. What is called here society is composed of so small a number of persons, that to break up into factions would be fatal. In all public places one is sure of meeting the same three hundred faces, from which results a more amusing and infinitely less hypocritical society than elsewhere.

It is the custom here to offer in return everything that is praised. At a recent dinner I sat next the Prime Minister's fair friend, who is as stupid as a cabbage and excessively stout. She displayed somewhat handsome shoulders, on which rested a garland with glass or metal acorns, and not knowing what to say to her, I praised both beads and shoulders, to which she replied: "*Todo ese a la disposicion de V.*"

PARIS, 1854. — You will find the Sydenham Crystal Palace a vast Noah's Ark, marvelous as to its collection of curious objects, but regarded from an artistic stand-point, perfectly ridiculous; yet there is something at once so grand and so

[1] In this country there is no chance of rising.

simple in its construction that one must go to England to form a conception of it. It is a toy costing twenty-five millions; a cage in which several churches might waltz; and to you who are *gourmande*, I recommend its dinners.

The last days I passed in London interested me. I met socially all the eminent politicians, and was present at the debates on the Supplies in the Houses of Lords and Commons, in which the most renowned orators spoke, but in my opinion very abominably. I have brought a pair of garters from London. I do not know with what Englishwomen keep up their stockings, nor how they procure this indispensable article, but I believe it to be a very difficult matter and very trying to their virtue. The shopman who gave me these garters blushed up to the eyes. All the charming things you say to me would be a delight if experience had not taught me to distrust you. I dare not hope for what I desire so ardently. There is something very painful in conforming to your protocols, which, in point of contempt of logic and probability, are worthy of Nesselrode. I returned this morning from Caen. On my arrival there I proceeded to the hall of the Law School, where I found about two hundred men and a dozen ladies. I delivered my little discourse without the slightest emotion, being very civilly applauded. The ceremonies terminated with the reading of some rather good verses by a humpbacked dwarf, immediately after which I was conducted by the authorities to the *hôtel de ville*, where a banquet was given in my honor, at which excellent fish and delicious lobsters were enjoyed. At last the hoped-for moment of release came, when to my dismay the President of the Antiquaries arose, every one standing, and proposing my health, referred to me as remarkable in the three qualities of senator, a man of letters, and a scientist. Only the table separated us, and I was much inclined to throw a dish of rum jelly at his head. While he spoke I was meditating my reply, with no apparent possibility of finding a word. I returned thanks, however, in a speech of five minutes, with but a slight idea of what I was saying, which, however, I was assured was very eloquent. But my sufferings were nct over.

I was seized by the mayor and led to a concert of the Philharmonic Society, where I was exhibited to a large number of well dressed people, the women very fair and very pretty, attired much like Parisians except in a less lavish display of shoulders, and in wearing maroon colored half boots with their ball dress.

INNSPRUCK, *August*, 1854. — I am intoxicated with magnificent landscapes and panoramas. From Basle to Schaffhausen, on the right hand and left, are enchanting mountains, far finer than those of the lower Rhine so much admired by Englishwomen. At Constance we had capital trout and heard Tyroleans play on the *zitther*. Thence to this place we have traversed a region of forests, lakes, and mountains of increasing beauty and grandeur, but are overcome with fatigue such as one experiences after examining a fine picture gallery. I am recruiting here with delicious woodcock and extraordinary soups. The drawback of the journey lies in an ignorance of the manners and ideas of the people, far more interesting to me than all the landscapes. In the Tyrol the women seem to be treated according to their merit. They are harnessed to wagons and easily draw heavy loads, are excessively ugly, with enormous feet; and the ladies whom I met on the railway and boats are not much better. They wear indecent bonnets, sky-blue boots with apple-green gloves. It is in great part the above peculiarities that constitute what the natives call *gemüth*, and of which they are exceedingly vain. It strikes me that the radical deficiency in the works of art of this country is that of imagination, upon which, nevertheless, they pique themselves, falling consequently into the most pretentious extravagances.

PRAGUE, *September*, 1854. — This city is exceedingly picturesque and there is admirable music. Yesterday I strolled through several gardens and public concerts, and saw the national dances performed decently and soberly; while nothing can be more captivating than a Bohemian orchestra. The physique here differs much from that of Germany; very large heads, broad shoulders, very small hips, and no legs whatever—that is a picture of Bohemian beauty. We have exhausted our knowledge of anatomy in striving to understand how these women walk. They have, however, fine black eyes, very long and fine black hair, but feet of a length, thickness, and breadth to surprise travellers accustomed to the most extraordinary sights. Crinoline is unknown. At the public gardens in the evening they drink a bottle of beer, after which they take a cup of coffee, which disposes them to partake of three veal cutlets with ham, the interstices being filled up with some light pastry cakes resembling our buns. The blanket of my bed of various pretty colors, is one metre long, to which is buttoned a napkin that serves me for sheet, and when I have arranged that in equilibrium, my servant places over the whole an eider down coverlet which I pass the night in throwing down and replacing.

VIENNA, *October*, 1854.—Really, this good city is an agreeable place of sojourn, and it requires a certain degree of courage to leave it, now that I have learned to enjoy sauntering about its pleasant places, and have made many friends. We are agitated by news from the Crimea. Is Sebastopol taken? It is believed so here; and the Austrians, with the exception of a few ancient families who are Russian at heart, congratulate us. God grant that the news may not be an invention such as the telegraph delights in when at leisure. However it may be, I think it a fine thing that our troops, six days after landing, should have pommeled the Russians so vigorously. We enjoy the looks of the Russians now here. Prince Gortschakoff says that it is an "incident" that will effect no change as to principles. The Belgian Minister, the wit of Vienna, says that Gortschakoff is right to intrench himself behind principles, because they are never taken with the bayonet. *À propos* of wit, willing or unwilling, I have been made a *lion*. Society here being so *gemüthlich*, everything that a Frenchman says is accepted as wit. I am thought very amiable. I write sublime thoughts in albums, I make drawings, in a word I have been perfectly ridiculous. I passed three days at Pesth, where my modesty suffered in being shown a public bath, in which Hungarian men and women were together in the hot mineral water. I saw one beautiful Hungarian who hid her face with her hands ; in this unlike the Turkish women, who wear the chemise for that purpose. I have heard Bohemian musicians play very original Hungarian airs that intoxicate the natives. The music begins lugubriously and ends with a mad gayety that quickly spreads to the audience, who stamp, break the glasses, and dance on the table ; but foreigners are not affected by these phenomena. Magnificent furs are obtained here for a trifle — the only bargains in the country. I am ruined by hack hire and dinner parties. The custom is to pay the domestics who serve the dinner, and the hall porter ; in fact one pays at every turn.

LONDON, *July*, 1856. — I am about to visit a real Scotch chieftain, who has never worn any breeches, has no staircase in his house, but maintains a bard and a seer. I find the people here so amiable, so pressing, so monopolizing, that my arrival is evidently a relief to their *ennui*. Yesterday I saw two of my former beauties ; the one has become asthmatic, the other a Methodist. I have also made the acquaintance of eight or ten poets, who struck me as rather more ridiculous even than our own.

EDINBURGH. — I have passed three days at the Duke of Hamilton's, in an immense castle, and a very fine country. At no great distance is a herd of wild oxen, said to be the only ones now remaining in Europe, but which appeared to me as tame as the deer at Paris. Throughout this castle are pictures by the great masters, magnificent Greek and Chinese vases, and richly bound books from the greatest collections of the last century. All this is arranged without taste, and one sees that it affords the proprietor but small enjoyment. I now understand why the French are so much in request in foreign countries; they take pains to be amused, and in so doing amuse others. I found myself the most entertaining person of the very numerous society assembled, and was at the same time conscious of being rather the reverse. I find Edinburgh altogether to my taste with the exception of the execrable architecture of the monuments, the claim of which to be Greek is about as well founded as an Englishwoman's pretension to be a Parisian because her toilettes are prepared by Madame Vignon. The accent of the natives is odious to me. The women, as a rule, are very ugly. The country necessitates short skirts, and they conform to the fashion and to the exigencies of the climate, by holding up their gown with both hands, a foot above the petticoat, displaying sinewy legs and half-boots of rhinoceros leather, with feet to match. I am shocked at the proportion of red-haired women whom I meet.

August, 1856, *at a country house near Glasgow.*—I lead a pleasant life, going from château to château, and everywhere entertained with a hospitality for which I despair of finding adequate expression, and which is only practicable in this aristocratic country. I am contracting bad habits. The guest here of poor people who have little more than thirty thousand pounds a year, I have thought myself not sufficiently honored because of dining without wind instruments and a piper in grand costume.

At the Marquis of Breadalbane's I passed three days in driving about the park. There are about two thousand deer, besides eight or ten thousand in his forests not adjacent to the castle. There are also, for the sake of singularity, at which every one aims here, a herd of American buffaloes, very fierce, inclosed in a peninsula, and which one goes to look at through the palings. Every one there, Marquis and buffalo, had the air of being bored. I believe that their pleasure consists in making people envious, and I doubt whether this compensates for the pother of playing innkeeper to all sorts of people. Amidst all this luxury, I observe, from time to time, bits of stinginess which amuse me.

KINLOCH-LINCHARD, *August*, 1856.—I begin to be satiated with grouse and venison. The truly remarkable scenery has still a charm for me, but my curiosity is satisfied. What I am not weary of admiring is, the bristling attitude the people here maintain: being chained together at the galleys even would not make them more sociable. This arises from their fear of being "caught in the act of being stupid," as Beyle says, or rather an organization that inclines them to prefer selfish pleasures. We arrived here at the same time with two gentlemen and a middle-aged woman accustomed to high society, and who had travelled. At dinner the thick ice necessarily thawed; but in the evening the husband took up a newspaper, the wife a book, the other gentleman began to write letters, while I was left to play a single-handed game against my hosts. I am told that the Celtic race (who live in frightful holes near the palace in which I am a guest) know how to talk. The fact is, I fancy, that on market day a continual noise of animated voices, laughter and shouts, is heard. Gælic is very soft. In England and the Lowlands, complete silence.

CARABACEL, *December*, 1856.—I have been besieged by Russian and English cards, and have been offered a presentation to the Grand Duchess Helen, an honor that I pointedly declined. To furnish us with gossip we have a Countess Apraxine, who smokes, wears round hats, and keeps a goat in her *salon*, which she has strewn with grass. But the most amusing person is Lady Shelley, who commits some fresh drollery every day. Yesterday she wrote to the French Consul: "Lady S—— informs M. P—— that she has a charming dinner party of English people to-day, and she will be delighted to see him afterwards, at five minutes past nine o'clock." She wrote to Madame Vigier, ex-Mademoiselle Cruvelli: "Lady Shelley would be charmed to see Madame Vigier if she would be good enough to bring her music with her." To which the ex-Cruvelli immediately replied: "Madame Vigier would be charmed to see Lady Shelley, if she would be good enough to come to her house and behave as a lady."

LONDON, *British Museum*, 1858. — You can form no conception of the beauty of the Museum on Sunday when there is no one present except M. Panizzi and myself; it seems to be permeated by a marvelous atmosphere of thought. Last Wednesday I fell into rather a droll scrape. I was invited to the Literary Fund dinner presided over by Lord Palmerston, and at the moment of setting out was notified that I should be expected to make a speech, as my name would be associated with a toast to the literature of Continental Europe. I was victimized with a satisfaction that you may imagine, and during fifteen minutes uttered nonsense in bad English before an assemblage of three hundred literary men, and a hundred women admitted to the honor of seeing us eat stringy chickens and tough tongue. I have never been so saturated with foolishness, as Pourceaugnac says.

Yesterday I received a visit from a gentleman and wife who brought me a number of autograph letters from Napoleon to Josephine, which they wished to sell. They are exceedingly curious in the fact of touching on nothing but love, and are doubtless authentic; but it is difficult to understand why Josephine did not burn them as soon as read.

PALACE OF FONTAINEBLEAU, *May*, 1858. — I am excessively annoyed and half poisoned from having taken too much laudanum; in addition to which, I have written verses for His Majesty of the Netherlands, played charades, and "made a fool of myself" generally. Shall I describe the life we lead here? Yesterday we took a stag and dined on the grass; the other day we were all drenched with rain; every day we eat too much, and I am completely exhausted. Destiny did not fashion me for a courtier. I shall try to snatch a little sleep while awaiting the fatal hour of getting under arms, which is to say, donning tights. How much I should prefer to stroll through this fine forest with you, chatting of fairy-land. I am exceedingly vexed with your ridiculous prudery. The book in question has the misfortune to be badly written, that is to say, in an enthusiastic tone that Sainte-Beuve extols as poetic, so much do tastes differ. One does not, when possessed of your taste, exclaim that it is frightful, immoral, but finds all that is good in the volume very good. You allow your prejudices to sway your judgment, and each day you grow more prudish, more in consonance with the affectation of the age. Your crinoline I overlook, but not your prudery.

VENICE, *August*, 1858. — Venice filled me with sadness. I have been moved to indignation by all the commonplaces uttered of the architecture of the palaces, which is effective, but destitute of taste and imagination. The canals resemble the Bièvre, and the gondola an inconvenient hearse. The pictures of the second-rate masters at the Academy pleased me; but there is not a Paul Veronese worth "The Marriage of Cana," not a Titian to be compared with "Christ with the Tribute Money" at Dresden, or even "The Crown of Thorns" at Paris. On the other hand, I am pleased with the physiognomy of the people. The streets swarm with charming girls with bare feet and head, who, if bathed and scrubbed, would serve as models for the Venus Anadyomene. I was present at an amusing *funzione* in honor of the Archduke. A serenade was given, six hundred gondolas following the colossal boat that carried the music, all bearing lanterns and burning red and blue Bengal lights, which touched the palaces on the grand canal with a magical tint. In passing the Rialto no gondola would draw back, nor give way, so that the mass formed a solid bridge, and at every moment was heard the crash of collision and breaking oars; but an observable feature was, that amid all the excitement of the throng, which in France would have led to a general battle, no abusive language was heard, not even a cross word. These people are made of milk and maize. To-day I saw a monk, in the middle of St. Mark's Square, fall on his knees before an Austrian corporal about to arrest him. There was never any thing more pitiable, and in front of the lion of St. Mark!

In a pretty villa on the banks of Lake Como I saw Madame Pasta, whom I had not met since her palmy days at the Italian

Opera. She has singularly increased in size, cultivates cabbages, and says that she is as happy as when crowns and sonnets showered on her. We discussed the theatre, music, and she remarked, justly, that since Rossini, no opera had been composed in which there was unity of thought and treatment.

CHÂTEAU DE COMPIÈGNE, *November*, 1858. — This morning I saw my friend Sandeau in the frame of mind natural to one who has appeared in knee-breeches the first time. He asked me a hundred questions with a *naiveté* that alarmed me. We have had great men from over the Channel, Russians and the Ministers, but the greater part of the guests took their departure yesterday, and we are left *en petit comité*, that is to say, we are but thirty or forty at table. One cannot sleep in this place. The time is passed in being frozen or roasting, and this has given me an irritation of the chest that exhausts me. But it is impossible to imagine a more amiable host or a more gracious hostess. When I think that I could have seen you to-day in Paris, I am tempted to fly from here ; and also to hang myself at your resignation: a virtue that I do not possess, and which enrages me in others. Nothing is easier here than to absent one's self from breakfast, or the morning walk, but dinner is the momentous ceremony; and when I spoke to the old courtiers of my intention to dine in town, they frowned in such evident consternation that I saw it must not be thought of.

CANNES, *January*, 1859. — There are great numbers of English here. I dined yesterday with Lord Brougham and I know not how many Misses freshly arrived from Scotland, whom the sight of the sun appeared greatly to surprise. Had I the talent to describe costumes, I could amuse you with those of these ladies ; you have never seen anything to parallel it since the invention of crinoline.

I have just read the Memoirs of Catherine II., which present a strange picture of the people and courts of that period.

Catherine on her marriage with the Grand Duke, afterwards Peter III., had a quantity of diamonds and superb brocaded robes, and for her lodgings a chamber that served as a passageway for her women, who, to the number of seventeen, slept in a single room next that of the queen. There is not to-day a grocer's wife who does not live more comfortably than the empresses of a hundred years ago. Catherine gives us sufficient strong reasons for believing Paul I. to be the son of Prince Soltikoff; and the curious thing is, that the manuscript in which she narrates these fine histories was addressed to her son, this same Paul, an animal for whom strangling was the best mode of suppression. I am glad that my critique on Mr. Prescott has pleased you. I am not altogether satisfied with it as I only expressed half of what I should like to say, acting on the aphorism of Philip II.: that one must say only good of the dead. In fact, the work is only of slight interest, and not above mediocrity. It strikes me that had the author been less Yankee, he could have done something better. We have marvelous moonlight, the sea like glass, and the heat of June. I am more and more convinced that heat is my great restorative. When it rains I have horrible spasms: as soon as the sun returns Richard is himself again. Cannes is becoming too civilized: one of the loveliest walks is to be destroyed for the railway; we shall become the prey of Marseilles, and the picturesque will be lost.

PARIS, *April*, 1859. — The war in Italy will be sharp, but not long; the financial state of the world could not allow it; and after the first shock I hope that England will intervene. Austria has no money, and many persons believe her motive to be simply a pretext for declaring her bankruptcy. Our people are warlike and confident, the soldiers gay and sanguine. There is an enthusiasm, a buoyancy in our army, in which the Austrians are totally deficient. Little of an optimist as I may be, I have full faith in our success. Our reputation is so well established that those who fight against us enter into it with little heart. A Russian alliance is still spoken of, in which I have no faith, for Russia has nothing to lose in the quarrel, and however it may terminate she will find it to be to her advantage: meanwhile she amuses herself with panslavist intrigues among the Austrian subjects, who regard the Emperor Alexander as their Pope. The Austrians are said to wear a modest, somewhat shamefaced air. The mass of our people are intensely interested and offer vows for success. The *salons*, especially those of the Orleanists, are perfectly anti-French and arch fools, who imagine that they will float back with the tide, and that their burgraves will resume the thread of their discourse that was snapped in 1848. Poor people! who do not understand that after this will come division, a republic, and anarchy. Germany is bawling against us; a mere jet of underlying red liberalism which just now assumes the Teutonic form. Russia is a terrible ally who would devour Germany, but who would gain for us England's ill-will, and perhaps hostility. We have so long led a sybaritic life as to ignore the emotions of our fathers; but we must now return to their philosophy. Our troops, rest assured, will be well taken care of, and will eat *macaroni stupendi* while the Austrians will sometimes find verdigris in their soup. Were I a young man, an Italian campaign would be to me the most attractive way of seeing a spectacle always noble — the awaking of an oppressed people.

PARIS, *May*, 1859. — Germany is still fermenting, which will result, apparently, rather in beer drinking than in blood shedding. Prussia resists to her utmost the pressure of the *Franzosenfresser*, and proclaims her intention to retake not only Alsace, but also the German provinces of Russia. This last jest would indicate that this Teutonic enthusiasm is neither serious nor well-considered. M. Yvan Tourguenieff, who comes direct from Moscow, says that all Russia is offering prayers for us, and that the army would be delighted to have a brush with the Austrians, whom, the priests are preaching, God will punish for their persecution of the orthodox Greeks of the Sclavonic race; and subscriptions are open to send

Sclavonic Bibles and tracts to the Croats to preserve them from papal heresy. This looks very like a political propaganda of panslavism.

A strong attack is now being organized against the Derby Ministry. Lord Palmerston and Lord John would be reconciled — rather an improbable event — or still more unlikely would unite for the destruction of the present Cabinet. The radicals will support them. Whatever may be the issue, we shall gain little by the change. Lord Palmerston, though the main promoter of the Italian agitation, would no more uphold it than would Lord Derby, only he would treat Austria with less consideration and would not seek to embarrass us. The wiseacres announce that all Europe will intervene: not improbable; but after the famous phrase *Sin all' Adriatico*, how can we leave Italy only half-delivered? How hope that a young emperor, suckled and governed by the Jesuits, beaten and in a bad humor, should confess his folly and ask pardon! Would not the Italians, who until now have been circumspect, be goaded into every imaginable imprudence pending the negotiations?

PARIS, *July*, 1859. — You alone reconcile me to the Peace. Perhaps it was necessary; but on the whole what matters to us the liberty of a parcel of smokers and musicians? We heard this evening the Emperor's speech, which was well delivered, with a grand air, an air of frankness and good faith: there is sense and truth in it. The returning officers say that the Italians are brawlers and cowards; that only the Piedmontese can fight, who, however, pretend that we were in their way, and that without us they could have done better. The Empress asked me in Spanish what I thought of the speech; to which I replied, combining candor with courtesy: "*Muy necesario.*"

PARIS, 1859. — I am reading the "Letters of Madame du Deffand." They are very amusing, giving an excellent picture of the society of her day, which was very amiable and somewhat frivolous. A striking contrast to the present era is manifest in their general and earnest endeavor to please ; as also in the sincerity and fidelity of their affections. They were more obliging people than ourselves, and especially than you, whom I no longer love.

PARIS, *September*, 1859. — The other day I met Edmond About, who is always charming. He resides at Saverne and passes his life in the woods, where a month ago he encountered a singular animal walking on all fours, wearing a black coat and varnished boots without soles. It proved to be a professor from Angoulême, who had been driven to the Baden gambling table by conjugal unhappiness, where he lost everything. Returning to France through the forests he missed his way and had eaten nothing for eight days. About carried and dragged him to a village where he was supplied with linen and food, but he survived only a short time. When the man-animal lives in solitude for a certain period, and reaches a certain state of physical dilapidation, it appears that he walks on all fours. About assures me that this *chef-d'œuvre* makes a very ugly animal.

You are growing stout and brown with the sun : but however you may be, fat or thin, I shall love you always tenderly. I have frightful spasms, am still ill, and suspect that I am on the great railway leading beyond the tomb. At some moments this thought is painful, at others I find the consolation that one experiences on the railway — the absence of responsibility in the presence of a superior and irresistible power.

PARIS, *September*, 15, 1859. — I was summoned from Tarbes by letter to Saint-Sauveur to pass the day, my visit being returned by their majesties ; which occasioned a great disturbance in M. Fould's household, Madame Fould improvising a dinner and breakfast, taxing to the utmost the resources of the little village. Their majesties were in excellent health and capital spirits at Saint-Sauveur, and I admired the natives, who had the good taste to leave them entirely to themselves. The

Emperor has bought a dog rather larger than a donkey, of the ancient Pyrenean breed: a magnificent brute which climbs rocks like a chamois.

MADRID, *October*, 1859. — Everything here is changed. The ladies whom I left as thin as spindles have become elephants, the climate of Madrid having a very fattening quality. Not only the manners, but the picturesque aspect of old Spain are notably altered by politics and a parliamentary government. At this moment nothing is discussed but war, the question of avenging the national honor exciting a general enthusiasm that recalls the Crusades. It is imagined that the English view the African expedition with displeasure and even wish to prevent it, which redoubles the warlike ardor. The army wish to lay siege to Gibraltar, after taking Tangiers!

CANNES, 1860. — Baron Bunsen is here with his two daughters, both mounted on crane's feet, with ankles resembling the club of Hercules; one of the young ladies, however, sings very well. Bunsen is clever enough and knows the news, of which you keep me but ill-informed. I have read the pamphlet by Abbé ——, which strikes me as even more clumsy than violent. He must be thought an *enfant terrible* at Rome, where neither good sense nor finesse is lacking, and where the priests are skillful intriguers. Ours have the national blustering instinct, and are devoid of tact.

Here is a nice little incident characteristic of this region. A farmer in the neighborhood of Grasse is found dead in a ravine where he had fallen or been thrown during the night. Another farmer comes to see a friend and tells him that he has killed the man. "How? and why?" "Because he cast a spell over my sheep; then I asked the advice of my shepherd, who gave me three needles to boil in a pot, over which I pronounced the words he taught me. The same night that I put the pot on the fire the man died." Do not be surprised should my books be burned in the church square at Grasse.

The recent brochure by my colleague Villemain, is singularly vapid. When one has attempted to write a book against the Jesuits, and has boasted of being the defender of liberty of conscience against the omnipotence of the Church, it is droll to hurl forth a recantation and to support it by such feeble argument. I believe that every one has gone mad, except the Emperor, who reminds one of the shepherds of the Middle Ages whose magic flute inspired the wolves to dance. I am seriously told that the French Academy, which has been markedly Voltairian these few years past, wishes to nominate Abbé Lacordaire as a protest against the violence to which the Pope is subjected. The matter is really one of perfect indifference to me. So long as I shall not be compelled to listen to their sermons, all the members of the Sacred College may be nominated to the Academy.

I have been on a little excursion in the region of eternal snow, where I saw fine rocks, cascades, and precipices, and a great subterranean cavern of unknown extent, supposed to be inhabited by all the gnomes and devils of the Alps. In fact, I passed a week in the enjoyment of pure nature and lumbago. We have here a Siberian wind, and this morning some snowflakes fell before my window; an unheard-of scandal in the memory of the oldest inhabitant of Cannes. I am ill, melancholy, wearied. My sight is failing and I can no longer sketch. What a sad thing is this growing old! Bulwer's novel, "What will he do with it?" appears to me senile to the last degree; nevertheless it contains some pretty scenes and has a very good moral. As to the hero and heroine, they transcend in silliness the limits of romance. A book that has amused me is a work by M. de Bunsen on the origin of Christianity and on *everything*, to speak more exactly; but it styles itself: "Christianity and Mankind." M. de Bunsen, though calling himself a Christian, has little respect for the Old and New Testaments.

PARIS, *May*, 1860. — The ball at the Hôtel d'Albe was superb; the costumes were very fine, many of the women very pretty, and typifying the audacity of the age being *décolletées* in the most outrageous fashion both as to skirt and waist.

During the waltz I saw a number of charming feet and many garters. Crinoline is declining. Be assured that within two years dresses will be worn very short, and the natural advantages of those so fortunate as to possess them will be distinguished from artificial charms. Some of the Englishwomen passed belief. The captivating daughter of Lord —— represented a Dryad, or some mythological personage, in a dress that would have left the entire bust exposed but for the semi-veil of a sort of swaddling band. It was nearly as conspicuous as the scanty drapery of the Mamma. The *ballet* of the Elements was danced by sixteen quite pretty women in short petticoats and covered with diamonds. The Naiads were powdered with silver, which, falling on their shoulders, resembled drops of water. The Salamanders were powdered with gold; one among them, Mademoiselle Errazu, being wondrously beautiful. The Princess Mathilde, painted a deep *bistre*, personated a Nubian, and was much too exact in costume. In the midst of the ball, a domino embraced Madame S——, who uttered loud screams. The dining-room with its surrounding gallery, the servants in their dresses as pages of the sixteenth century, and the electric light, recalled Martin's picture of Belshazzar's Feast. The Emperor changed his domino in vain; he would have been recognized at a league distant. The Empress wore a white bournous and black velvet mask, which did not disguise her in the least. There were many foolish dominos; the Duc de —— walking about as a tree,—an excellent imitation. At the ball given by M Aligre, a wife was pinched black and blue by her ferocious husband. The wife screamed and fainted; general tableau! The jealous idiot was not thrown out of the window, which would have been the only sensible thing to do. At a recent masked ball a lady had the temerity to appear in a costume of 1806, without crinoline, which produced a great sensation. These are fine commentaries on the times and women.

An amusing incident occurred lately. M. Boitelle, Prefect of Police, who should certainly be the best informed man in Paris, learned through the reports of faithful agents that M.

Fould, the Minister of State, had gone to sleep in his newly built house in the Faubourg Saint-Honoré. Very early in the morning the Prefect appeared, pressed the Minister's hand very demonstratively, explaining the important part he had taken in what had just occurred. M. Fould thought that he referred to his son, who is committing follies in England. This *quid pro quo* lasted until the Prefect asked permission to know the name of his successor in the Cabinet, to which M. Fould replied, that he had come to his new residence merely as a house-warming, and had found it more convenient to sleep there than at the Ministerial palace.

It appears that Lamoricière is already somewhat weary of the imbroglio that greets him in the papal territory. Cardinal Antonelli remarked a short time ago to a foreign minister, that he had never met a man of more comprehensive mind than Lamoricière. "I have discussed the intricate situation of affairs with him, for which he immediately suggested five or six remedies ; and he talks so well, that within the hour he gave me four different opinions on the same question, all so strongly fortified that I am perplexed as to a choice." Every one here is preoccupied by Garibaldi's expedition, which will, it is feared, result in a general complication. Should he break his back in Sicily, I think that perhaps M. de Cavour would not be too much distressed, but if he succeed, he will become ten times more dangerous.

Read Granier de Cassagnac's book on the Girondins. Portions of it are exceedingly curious, and it presents a horrible picture of the massacres and revolutionary atrocities ; all written with much fire and vigor. Three days ago I received a visit from M. Feydeau, who is a very fine fellow, but artlessly betrays an extreme vanity. He is going to Spain to complement what Cervantes and Lesage have merely outlined ! He has still thirty romances to write, the scene of which will be laid in thirty different countries ; this is why he travels. I think of you incessantly in spite of your faults.

PARIS, *July*, 1860. — The funeral of Prince Jerome was a terrible ceremony. I do not know how many vacancies it has created in our ranks, but fear that only the undertakers have profited by it. More than thirty thousand persons came to sprinkle holy water, which shows the flunkyism of this high-minded nation! It is even more senseless than is supposed, and that is saying much. You lost a fine spectacle, that of seeing me, *in fiocchi* and black gloves, pass through the Rue de Rivoli amid the admiring populace. We were one hour and three quarters in defiling between the Palais Royal and the Invalides, then came the mass, then the funeral oration by Abbé Cœur, who praised the principles of '89, while declaring our soldiers to be ready to die in defense of the Pope. He also said that the first Napoleon had no love for war, but was always forced to the defensive. The finest part of the ceremony was a *De profundis* chanted in the vault, and which we heard through black crape that separated us from the grave. Were I a musician I would profit in opera by the admirable effect of this crape in modifying sound.

The Orleanists pretend that M. Brénier has been knocked in the head by an uncivil husband; but the more credible rumor is that the lazzaroni have thus sought to avenge the violence offered to their king. The liberals, in retaliation, have assassinated the police, which has been of much benefit to M. Brénier. The northern Italians have not the quick sensibility of the Neapolitans. They have logic and common sense, as Stendhal said, while the Neapolitans are merely badly trained children.

In the evening every one goes to the Champs-Elysées to hear Musard's music; fine ladies and *lorettes* mingled pell-mell, and are difficult to distinguish one from the other. And people go to the circus to see the learned dogs roll a ball up an inclined plane by leaping on it! This generation is losing all taste for intellectual pleasures.

SOUTH PARADE, BATH, *August*, 1860. — Such a life as mine here would make a thorough-bred horse broken-winded:

in the morning, walks, shopping, and visiting; in the evening, dinners with the aristocrats, where I always find the same dishes and nearly the same faces. I could hardly remember the names of my hosts, for in their white cravats and black coats, all Englishmen look very much alike. We are extremely detested here, and still more dreaded. Nothing is more droll than the fear they have of us, which they are at no pains to disguise. The volunteers are even more stupid than the National Guard was with us in 1830; for in this country everything is invested with an air of gravity not to be seen elsewhere. I know a very honest fellow sixty years of age, who drills every day in Zouave breeches. The Ministry is very weak and does not know its own mind, and the Opposition is not more wise. But great and small agree in believing that we covet general annexation. At the same time, there is no one who supposes a war to be possible, unless the question of annexing the three kingdoms should be agitated. I am not very well pleased with the Emperor's letter to M. de Persigny. It would have been much better in my opinion, to say nothing at all, or simply to tell them what I repeat every evening: that they are great fools.

LONDON, 18 *Arlington Street*, 1860. — Only after some time in London do I accustom myself to its singular light, which seems to pass through brown gauze, the effect being that of an eclipse. This atmospheric peculiarity and the curtainless windows will annoy me for some days to come; but on the other hand I am regaling on all manner of good things, breakfasting and dining like an ogre.

It is evident that the affairs of the East are becoming more complicated every moment. The disembarking of the French in Syria would be followed by a general explosion of massacre and pillage throughout the East; very probably, also, the Turkish provinces of Greece — that is to say, Thessaly, Macedonia, and Christian Albania — would be excited to retaliation. Everything will be on fire this winter in the East, and to visit Algeria at such a moment seems to me perfect madness. The "Times" to-day announces four feet of snow at Inverness. Shall I find enough charcoal and plaids in Scotland to remedy this evil?

GLENQUOICH, *August*, 1860. — The weather here is always detestable, but it does not hinder people from going out. They are so accustomed to rain, that unless it be of extraordinary violence they are not deterred from walking. The paths are sometimes torrents, and the mountains are invisible within a hundred paces; but these people return, saying "Beautiful walk." One of the greatest annoyances of this region is a little fly called midge, which is exceedingly venomous; and though there are two young ladies here, the one blonde, the other red-haired, and both with skin of satin, these horrible insects prefer to attack me. Our chief amusement is fishing, and fortunately the insects do not venture on the lake. There are fourteen persons here. During the day each one goes his own way; in the evening, after dinner, each one takes a book or writes letters. To chat and seek to amuse each other is a thing unknown to the English. The Highland air has benefited me, and I breathe more easily. Our hunters kill deer and grouse; and every day we have excellent birds; but I cannot eat, the main pleasure amid this rain and fog; and I sigh for a *soupe maigre*, or for a solitary dinner at home, or with you at Saint-Cheron: this last wish will never be realized, I fear.

PARIS, *September*, 1860. — Panizzi has been with me for ten days, and I am acting cicerone, showing him everything, from cedar to hyssop. I understand nothing of the disorders that have begun. My guest thinks that the Pope and the Austrians will be driven out. For the first, appearances are unfavorable; as to the others, I believe that if Garibaldi meddles with them he will burn his fingers. From Naples comes a royal philosophical witticism. Previous to embarking, His Majesty received, every five minutes, the resignation of a General or an Admiral: "Now they are too thoroughly Italians to fight against

Garibaldi ; a month hence they will be too much of royalists to fight against the Austrians." It would be impossible for you to imagine the fury of the Orleanists and Carlists. A rather sensible Italian tells me that M. de Cavour caused the Sardinian army to enter the States of the Church, because Mazzini was about to incite a revolution there.

I hear that the *fêtes* at Marseilles in the Imperial honor were very fine : that the enthusiasm was at once deliberate and clamorous, and that perfect order was maintained notwithstanding the immense, overexcited Southern multitude. The spectacle of the Marseillaise, in their ordinary state, is always sufficiently amusing, but, when under excitement, they must be still more absurd. But they not only lost their heads on the occasion of the Emperor's visit, but also two barrels of Spanish wine that I have been expecting. The merchant who should have received them writes to me very naïvely, that he was too much occupied with the *fêtes* to think of my wine, and could only attend to it after taking a little rest.

I lately passed a few days at Saintonge, where I found every one discomfited, weeping their eyes away for the misfortunes of the Holy Father and General Lamoricière. It is said that General Changarnier is writing a narrative of his colleague's campaign, in which, after bestowing the highest eulogies, he proves that Lamoricière committed the most enormous follies. In my opinion, the only one of the martyr heroes at whom one cannot laugh, is Pimodan, who died like a brave soldier. Those who exclaim against the martyrs because they have been taken, move me to no pity. Moreover, the present time is perfectly comic ; and it is comfortable to learn every morning, through one's paper, of a catastrophe, to read Cavour's notes and the encyclicals. I see that they have shot Walker, in America, which surprises me, for his case is precisely that of Garibaldi whom we all admire.

Two evenings ago, wishing for some music, I went to the Italiens, where they gave the "Barber of Seville." This music, the gayest ever written, was executed by people with the air of having just returned from a funeral. Alboni, who played

Rosina, sang admirably, with the expression of a bird organ. Gardoni sang like a gentleman who fears to be mistaken for an actor. Had I been Rossini I should have beaten them every one. Only Basilio, whose name I do not recall, sang as if he understood the words.

I am told that the Empress, whom I have not yet seen, is still terribly afflicted. She sent me a fine photograph of the Duchesse d'Albe, taken twenty-four hours after death, which was very calm; she looks as if in a quiet sleep. Five minutes before her death she laughed at her waiting-maid's Valencian *patois*. I have no direct news of Madame de Montijo since her departure, but I fear that the poor lady will not bear up under this dreadful blow.

I am in the midst of academical intrigues; the question not one touching the French Academy, but that of the fine arts. An intimate friend of mine is the favored candidate, but he has received an intimation from His Majesty to give place to M. Haussmann, the Prefect. The Academy is annoyed, and wishes to nominate my friend in spite of himself, which I encourage to the utmost; and I should like to tell the Emperor the wrong he does himself in mingling with matters that do not concern him. I hope for success, and that the Colossus will be finely blackballed.

Italian affairs are very amusing, and what is said of them by the few honest people here is still more droll. The martyrs of Castelfidardo are beginning to arrive, among them a young man of eighteen years who allowed himself to be taken, and whose aunt I saw a few days ago. She said: "The Piedmontese behaved in an atrocious manner to my nephew." I awaited some appalling revelation. "Only imagine, Monsieur, five minutes after being made prisoner the poor fellow's watch was gone. A gold hunting watch that I had given him!"

October, 1860. — I quite understand that the first view of Oriental life should dazzle you. One sees things both droll and to be admired at every step; in fact, there is always something droll in Orientals as in certain strange, pompous beasts that we formerly saw at the Jardin des Plantes. Decamps has caught this ludicrous phase, but not the very fine, noble side of their character.

Thanks to your sex you are privileged to enter the harems and chat with the women. Do they in Algeria, as in Turkey, make a display of their charms? Tell me how they dress, what they say, and what they think of you. What is the character of the dances that you saw? Were they modest, and did you comprehend their sentiment? I imagine that they are more interesting than those of Parisian balls; and they probably resemble the dances of the gypsy women of Granada. I do not doubt that an Arab, from Sahara, in witnessing a waltz in Paris, would conclude, and naturally, that the Frenchwomen were enacting pantomime. In going to the root of things we always find the same primal ideas. Have you seen the women at the Moorish baths? I am inclined to believe that the habit of living with crossed legs must give them horrible knees. I suppose you will adopt kohl for your eyes, which is very pretty, being also, it is said, an excellent preservative against ophthalmia, an affection common and dangerous for European eyes in hot climates. I grant you my permission to try the effect. You give me sketches; I wish for details. There is nothing that you cannot say to me, and besides, you are renowned for your euphuisms. You have the art of academical expression. I congratulate you on your courage in learning Arabic. I once glanced through M. de Sacy's grammar and recoiled in terror, but I remember that there are lunar and solar letters, and I know not how many conjugations. My cousin, one of the most learned Arabists, who had passed twenty-five years at Djeddah, told me that he never opened a book without learning some new word, of which there were, for instance, five hundred for the one word lion.

PARIS, *October*, 1860. — I went to Saint-Cloud yesterday, where I breakfasted almost *tête-à-tête* with the Emperor, the Empress, and "Monsieur fils," as they say at Lyons. I talked a long while with the Emperor, principally of ancient history and Cæsar. He surprises me by the ease with which he comprehends erudite subjects, for which he has only recently acquired the taste. The Empress related some curious anecdotes of her journey to Corsica. The Bishop spoke to her of a bandit named Bosio, a thoroughly honest youth, whom the counsels of a woman had driven to commit several little murders. He is pursued for some months, but uselessly; women and children suspected of carrying him food are thrown into prison, but to lay hands on him is impossible. Her Majesty, who has read a certain romance,[1] became interested in this man, and said she should be very glad if he could be enabled to leave the island and go to Africa or elsewhere, where he might become a good soldier and an honest man. "Ah! Madame," said the Bishop, "will you allow me to have this told to him?" "How, Monseigneur, you know where he is?" General rule: the most worthless fellow in Corsica is always related to the most honest man. It greatly surprised the Imperial party that they should have been asked for a prodigious number of favors (*grâces*), but not for a sou; so the Empress returns full of enthusiasm.

The meeting at Warsaw is a failure. The Emperor of Austria invited himself, and was received with the politeness that is accorded to the indiscreet. Nothing of importance was accomplished. The Emperor of Austria essayed to prove that if Hungary was a source of danger to Austria, Russia had Poland; to which Gortschakoff replies: "You have eleven millions of Hungarians, and you are three millions of Germans. We are forty millions of Russians, and have no need of assistance in bringing six thousand Poles to their senses. Consequently, there is no necessity for mutual guaranties." England is calming down, and it is possible that she may make us overtures to adopt a joint policy with regard to Italy. In that event war would be impossible unless Garibaldi should attak Venice. They write me from Naples that the muddle is at its height, and the Piedmontese are expected there with

[1] Merimée's novel of *Colomba*.

the same impatience with which we in Paris in 1848 looked for the arrival of the troops of the line. They sigh for order and rest their hopes for its restoration on Victor Emmanuel alone. Moreover, Garibaldi and Alexandre Dumas have prepared their minds for peace, much in the same way as a a freezing rain disposes one to a hot dinner.

PARIS, *November*, 1860. — Affairs are still complicated by the condition of the East, which is such that our Ambassador at Constantinople expects the old machine to crack from top to bottom at any moment. The Sultan is selling his cachemires, and does not know if he will be able to buy a dinner next month. Do you know the Emperor Francis Joseph's greeting to the Emperor Alexander? "I bring you my guilty head!" The serf's formula on approaching his master in the fear of being beaten. This he said in good Russian, for he knows all languages. His servile meanness did not profit him much; Alexander preserved a most discouraging coldness, and the Prince Regent of Prussia, following his example, put on airs. After the departure of the Emperor Alexander, the Austrian emperor remained four hours alone at Warsaw, where there was no great Russian or Polish noblemen so poor to do him reverence. All this has been a great triumph to the old Russians, who detest the Austrians still more than the English or ourselves.

You have heard of our victory over these poor Chinese. What an absurdity to go so far for the purpose of killing people who have done us no harm. True, being a species of ourang-outang, the Grammont law alone can be invoked in their favor. I am preparing for our Chinese conquests by reading a new romance just translated by Stanislas Julien. It is the story of Mademoiselle Cân and Mademoiselle Ling, who are very witty, making verses and crambo on every occasion. They meet with two students possessing the same poetic facility, and a never-ending combat of quatrains ensues, the prominent idea of which is the blue lotus and white doves. It is impossible to conceive of any imaginative effort more uncouth and more barren of passion. The people who can be amused by this style of literature are evidently abominable pedants, who well deserve to be beaten and conquered by us, who are disciples of the noble Greek literature.

I dined to-day with Prince Napoleon. The Princess Clotilde admired my wrist buttons, and asked the address of my jeweler.

MARSEILLES, *November*, 1860.—My friend Mr. Ellice, of Glenquoich, will be my neighbor this winter. He has just purchased a Scotch estate next his own; or rather lakes, rocks, and heaths several leagues in extent. I cannot conceive what it will produce, unless it be grouse and deer.

I have brought with me a new edition of Pouschkine's works, and have promised to write a notice of him. I find magnificent things in his lyric poems, entirely after my own heart; that is to say, Greek in their truth and simplicity. I should like to translate several that are marked by great sprightliness, in which, as in precision and clearness, he strikes me as preëminent. One in the style of Sappho's ode reminds me that I am writing in the chamber of an inn, dreaming of happy moments in the past. I am ill and suffering; but of all petty miseries the worst for me is sleeplessness, when thoughts are gloomy, and one takes a dislike to one's self. The journey of the Empress to Scotland creates much gossip, and every one is mystified.

CANNES, *December*, 1860.—The political disturbance has somewhat agitated me, however unprejudiced in the premises I may be. You know how intimate I have been with the chief victim, M. Fould. As yet I know nothing positive respecting the reasons for his disgrace. It is evident, however, that a beautiful woman is somewhat implicated, who is anxious to dislodge him, and who has long sought to accomplish this end. M. Fould is less philosophical than I had thought, or than I should have been in his place; but he has been wounded by certain proceedings. As to the liberal measures, we must wait to see the result. As a principle, it is better to take the initiative in giving than to grant what has been long and impatiently demanded. On the other hand, the Emperor may be seeking support in the Chambers to enable him to withdraw from our false position in Italy, — protecting a Pope who excommunicated us *in petto*, while we risk a quarrel with our friends out of tenderness for the vanity of a puppet (the Emperor of Austria) who has never wished us well. Here, throughout France, the people who wear black coats and claim to be powerful are in favor of the Pope and the King of Naples, as if they had incited no revolution in France, but their love for the papacy and legitimacy does not stretch to the point of expending a crown for them. What will be the effect of the recrudescent eloquence with which the new concessions threaten us? The old Parliamentarians begin to prick up their ears. M. Thiers, it is said, will enter the lists as a candidate for the Deputies, and this example will be followed by many others. I can hardly imagine what will become of the Ministers without portfolio commissioned to represent the eloquence of the Legislative Body and the Senate; but it will be diverting to see orators like Messieurs Magne and Billault, with the Jules Favres and *tutti quanti.*

My friend Mr. Ellice is at Nice, whence he occasionally comes to visit me; he complains of finding no intellectual associates. I see that you have had a visit from Mr. Cobden, a man of talent and very interesting, the opposite of an Englishman, in that he never utters commonplaces and has few prejudices. I can give you no political news, for my correspondents tell me nothing, except that nothing is done. It is a characteristic of our generation to set out with a great hubbub that ends in loitering and amusing ourselves on the road.

CANNES, *February*, 1861. — I have been to Nice on a visit to my friend Mr. Ellice who is cruelly tortured by the gout. I confess to an involuntary sentiment of satisfaction in passing the bridge of the Var free from custom-house officers, gensdarmes, and passports. It is a fine annexation and makes one feel several millimetres taller.

M. Fould has been on a visit to me, and related many curious stories touching both men and women who intermeddled in his affairs. I doubt if he will have the courage to persevere in sulking. It appears that when one has carried a red portfolio under the arm for some time, the loss of it reduces him to the state of an Englishman without his umbrella.

If you find some pretty silk stuff that washes, and not too much like a woman's gown, order me a *robe de chambre* the longest possible, and buttoned down the left side, and in the Oriental fashion. Bring it with you, for I have no wish to wear silk gowns when the ice of the Seine is two feet thick. The cold reported at Paris makes my hair stand on end; nevertheless I am summoned there by the President. Do not be alarmed to see my illness announced. A dignity has been conferred on me which I could very well have dispensed with, but which compels me to be punctual; and they also write me that our Senate is papistical and legitimist, and that my vote will not be one too many for the ballot.

The poor Duchess of Malakof is an excellent person, not very bright, especially as to French. She appears to be entirely domineered over by her frightful monster of a husband, who is rough by habit and perhaps through policy. It is said, however, that she accommodates herself to the inevitable. Should you see her, speak of me and of our theatrical performances in Spain. I am told that her brother is an amiable fellow, very handsome, and a poet into the bargain. Thanks for the tobacco pouch, the gold and colored embroidery of which is exquisite. Only barbarians can do these things, our workmen having too much acquired art and not enough sentiment to equal them. Thanks also for the bananas, to my taste the most delicious fruit in the world.

PARIS, *March*, 1861. — Since my return to Paris I have been in a condition of utter stultification; first, as regards our exhibition at the Senate, where, I may say with M. Jourdain, I have been surfeited with nonsense. Every one had a speech prepared, that it was necessary to display, and so contagious was the example of dullness that I delivered my own like an idiot. I was cruelly frightened, but overcame it by reminding myself that I was in the presence of two hundred imbeciles, and with no reason for agitation. The joke of it was that M. Walewski, for whom I wished to obtain a satisfactory budget, was offended by my praise of his predecessor, and honestly declared that he would vote against my resolution. M. Troplong, near whom in virtue of my office as Secretary I was seated, condoled with me in a low tone; to which I replied that it was impossible to make a Minister drink who was not thirsty. This was repeated piping hot to M. Walewski, who took it for an epigram, and has frowned at me ever since.

The second *ennui* of the day is the official and private dinners, where one sees the same turbot, fillet, and lobster, and the same tiresome persons as on the preceding occasion. But the most irksome of all is Catholicism. You can hardly imagine the degree of exasperation to which Catholics are moved, flying in one's face for a mere nothing; for example, if one does not show the whites of one's eyes in hearing them discourse of the sainted martyr; and still more if one innocently inquires, as I have done, who has been martyrized. I have also got into a scrape in expressing astonishment that the Queen of Naples should be photographed in boots! — an exaggeration of my words and a surpassing stupidity. The other evening a lady asked me if I had seen the Empress of Austria. I said that I thought her very pretty. "Ah! she is ideal!" — No, it is an irregular face, more agreeable perhaps than if perfectly classical. — "Ah! Monsieur, she is beauty itself! Tears of admiration come to one's eyes!" And this is the society of to-day! I fly from it as from the plague. What has become of the French society of former years!

The latest, but a colossal bore, has been "Tannhauser." Some persons say that its representation at Paris was one of the secret clauses of the treaty of Villafranca; others, that Wagner has been given to us to compel our admiration of Ber lioz. The fact is, it is prodigious. I am convinced that I could write something similar if inspired by the scampering of my cat over the piano keys. The Princess de Metternich bestirred herself enormously in feigning to understand it and to lead the applause, which, however, never came. Every one yawned ; but at first the audience assumed the air of comprehending this keyless enigma. Beneath Madame de Metternich's box, it was said by the wits that the Austrians were taking their revenge for Solferino. It was also said that one wearies of the recitatives, and tires of the airs (*se tanne aux airs*). Try to catch the pun. Your Arabic music, I fancy, would be a capital preparation for this infernal uproar. The failure is stupendous ! Auber says that it is Berlioz without melody.

I am satisfied that within two months the Pope will either be off, or that we shall leave him to his own devices, or that he will come to some arrangement with Piedmont; but matters cannot remain in their present status. The bigots are raising a horrible outcry, but the Gallic *bourgeois* and the people are anti-papists.

You tell me nothing of your health, which appears to be good, nor of your complexion, which must be, I fear, somewhat browned.

PARIS, *May*, 1861. — You must have been sadly impressed with the aspect of winter in Central France, coming as you do from Africa. Whenever I return from Cannes I am horrified at the sight of the leafless trees and damp, dead earth.

The Catholics have rendered our *salons* insupportable. Not only have the former devotees become acid as verjuice, but all of the ex-Voltairians of the political opposition have turned papists. What consoles me, is, that some among them believe themselves obliged to attend mass, which must bore them sufficiently. My old Professor, M. Cousin, who formerly never spoke of the Pope but as the Bishop of Rome, is converted and never misses a mass. It is even said that M. Thiers is becoming devout, but I find some difficulty in believing it, for I have always had a weakness for him.

I am, at this very moment, a prey to the herrings that the sea-calves of Boulogne have raised up to torment us, and I await the Maronites as a finishing stroke — that is to say, we are disputing in the Senate, and very sharply, *à propos* to herrings, and we are menaced with daily sittings. Is it true that all the Boulogne herring fishers are thieves who buy the herrings taken by the English, and which they pretend to have caught themselves? Is it also true that the herrings have been seduced by the English, and pass no more along our coasts?

CHÂTEAU DE FONTAINEBLEAU, *June*, 1861. — I am resting under the trees with great happiness after my tribulations. Never have I seen men so enraged, so out of their senses as the magistrates. I console myself in thinking that if twenty years hence some antiquary shall burrow in the "Moniteur" of this week, he will say that one philosopher of moderation and calmness was found among an assembly of lunatics. This philosopher, without vanity, is myself. In this country magistrates are selected from men too stupid to gain their living as lawyers; they are badly paid, and are allowed to be crabbed and insolent. I have done my duty, and all is at an end. I was well received here, with no raillery on my defeat. I very clearly gave my opinion of the matter, and they do not appear to think me in the wrong. It is magnificent weather and the air of the forest is delicious. There are rocks and heather which would have their charms could I walk with you among them, chatting of all manner of things; but we go in a long file of *chars à bancs*, where one is not always well matched in point of capacity for amusing. There is not a republic, however, where one can have more freedom or find a host and hostess more amiable and kind to their guests. There are few people here. We have the Princess de Metternich, who is very animated after the German fashion, that is to say, she affects a species of originality composed of two parts *lorette*, one part great lady. I suspect that in reality there is not too much wit to sustain the *rôle* that she has adopted. One accomplishes nothing here. Sometimes I am summoned for a stroll in the woods; sometimes to make verses; but time is especially wasted in waiting. The great philosophy of the day is to know how to wait, and I have some difficulty in educating myself in the art. Thanks to Cæsar, doubtless, I shall be here until the end of the month. I am working for the *bourgeois* (the Emperor), with whom I am more pleased every day. I went last week to Alise with the Emperor, who is becoming an accomplished archæologist. He passed three hours and a half on the mountain, under the most terrific sun, examining the vestiges of Cæsar's siege, and reading the "Commentaries." We returned with the skin peeled from our ears, and the color of chimney-sweeps.

CHÂTEAU DE FONTAINEBLEAU, *June*, 1861. — We have had a capital ceremony here, reminding me of that in the "Bourgeois Gentilhomme." It was the most diverting spectacle possible, that of twenty black men exceedingly like monkeys, dressed in gold brocade with white stockings and varnished shoes, and swords at their side, all flat on their face and crawling on hands and knees the whole length of the Henri II. gallery, each one with his nose level with the back of the crawler preceding him. The hardest task fell to the first ambassador, who wore a felt hat embroidered in gold that danced on his head with each motion, and who held a bowl of gold filagree work within which were two boxes containing each a letter from their Siamese Majesties. The letters were inclosed in purses of gold-woven silk, the whole being very pretty. After delivering the letters to the Emperor, it became necessary to retire backward, and confusion fell upon the embassy. A succession of blows on the face of those behind them by the first rank, whose swords pierced the eyes of the second rank, who in turn made blind of one eye the third rank, was the result of this masterly retreat. They presented the appearance of a swarm of black beetles on the carpet. The Minister of Foreign Affairs had arranged the ceremony and exacted that the ambassadors should crawl, the effect of which moreover failed, for the Emperor at length lost all patience, rose, made the beetles rise, and spoke in English with one of them. The Empress kissed a little monkey whom they had brought, said to be the son of one of the ambassadors, who ran about on all fours like a little rat, but had an intelligent expression. The temporal king of Siam sent his portrait to the Emperor, and that of his wife, who is hideously ugly. You would be charmed by the beauty and variety of the stuffs they brought; gold and silver tissues so light and transparent as to resemble the clouds of a fine sunset. They gave the Emperor trowsers embroidered with ornaments in enamel and gold, and a vest of gold brocade as flexible as foulard, the designs, gold on gold, being really exquisite; while the buttons are of filagree gold, diamonds, and emeralds. They have a red gold and a white gold which produce an admirable effect when blended. In short, I have never seen anything at once so bewitching and splendid. The tastes of these savages is singular, in that their fabrics are not glaring although they use only brilliant silks, gold, and silver. All this is marvelously combined, producing on the whole a quiet and harmonious effect.

LONDON, *British Museum, July*, 1861. — You know, or you do not know, that there is a new Lord Chancellor, Lord B——, who is old, but his morals by no means so. A lawyer named Stevens sends his clerk with a card for the Chancellor; the clerk makes inquiries, and is told that my lord has no house in London, but that he often comes from the country to Oxford Terrace, where he has a temporary lodging. Thither the clerk proceeds and asks for my lord. "He is not here." "Do you think he will return for dinner?" "No, but to sleep certainly; he sleeps here every Monday." The clerk leaves the letter, and Mr. Stevens is greatly astonished that the Chancellor should look frightfully black at him. The gist of the story is, that my lord maintains a clandestine *ménage*.

I have not had a moment's rest since my arrival; dinner parties, balls, and concerts without cessation. Yesterday I attended a concert at the Marquis of Lansdowne's, where there was not a single pretty woman, a remarkable circumstance here; but, on the other hand, they were all dressed as if the first *modiste* of Brionde had composed their toilette. I have never seen anything to parallel their headdresses; one ancient dame, who wore a diamond crown composed of small stars with a huge sun in the centre, being an absolute counterpart of the wax figures that one sees at fairs!

Yesterday I dined at Greenwich with some great personages who exerted themselves to be lively, not like the Germans by throwing themselves from the windows, but by making an excessive noise. The dinner was abominably long, but the white bait excellent. We have unpacked two cases of antiquities just arrived from Cyrene. There are two statues and several remarkable busts, one of a good period and quite Greek; a Bacchus, that is especially captivating though with rather a mincing expression, the head being in an extraordinary state of preservation.

M. de Vidil is committed and will be tried at the next assizes. He is not admitted to bail, and the worst that can happen to him will be a sentence of imprisonment for two years; for where death does not supervene the English law does not recognize murder.

Lord Lyndhurst said to me that one must be extremely *maladroit* to be hung in England. I went the other evening to the House of Commons and heard the debate on Sardinia. Anything more verbose, more pointless (*gobe-mouche*), and fuller of bragadocio than the majority of the speakers it is impossible to imagine, and notably so Lord John Russell, now Earl Russell.

I have been interrupted by a visit to the Bank. They placed in my hand four small packages amounting to four million pounds sterling, but I was not allowed to bring them away. They showed me a very pretty machine that counts and weighs three thousand sovereigns per day. It hesitates a moment, and after a short deliberation throws the good sovereign to the right and the bad to the left. There is another that takes a bank bill, stoops and gives it, as it were, two little kisses, impressing on it marks that forgers have not as yet been able to imitate. Finally, I was conducted to the vaults, where I might have imagined myself in a grotto of the Arabian Nights; all filled with sacks of gold and ingots sparkling in the gaslight.

PARIS, *August*, 1861. — I do not know whether in consequence of too much turtle soup, or exposure to the sun, but I have again suffered from my former agonizing pains, which must resemble those of hanging, and which create in me no desire to be suspended. After six weeks of dinner parties I find it very comfortable not to don a white cravat. I passed a week in Suffolk County in a fine château, almost in solitude. It is a flat country, but covered with magnificent timber, with much water; it is very near the fens whence Cromwell came. The quantity of game is astonishing, and at every step one runs the risk of crushing partridges or pheasants.

Should Madame de Montijo go to Biarritz I shall join her and pass some days with her. She is inconsolable, and I find her even more sad than last year when her daughter died.

I see by your letter that you are as much occupied as a general-in-chief on the eve of battle. I remember reading in "Tristram Shandy," that in the house with a newly born babe all the women believe themselves entitled to tyrannize over the men; and I feared to be treated with the disdain inseparable from your present height of grandeur. For myself, I am but slightly inclined to love children; nevertheless, I can imagine that one may be attached to a little girl as to a kitten, an animal to which your sex bear a strong resemblance. There is perfect solitude here, by which I profit in preparing something promised to my master, and which I wish to take to Biarritz. I read little except Roman history; nevertheless, I have read M. Thiers's nineteenth volume with great pleasure. It strikes me as being written with greater negligence than its predecessors, but full of curious matter. In spite of his desire to speak ill of his hero, he is continually carried away by his involuntary love. He gives exceedingly amusing stories of Montrond, to whom I only regret not having related them while he was living. M. Thiers paints him correctly as an adventurer in love with his trade, and honest towards his employers during the period of his service, much the same as Dalgetty in the "Legend of Montrose."

BIARRITZ, *September*, 1861. — I am still here, dear friend, like a bird on a branch. It is not the custom here to make plans in advance, indeed they are resolved on only at the last moment. It is excessively cold after dinner, it being impossible to keep warm with the system of doors and windows that has been contrived here. The sea air is of service, and I breathe more easily, but sleep badly, as I am immediately on the shore, for the slightest wind rouses the waves to a terrific uproar. Time passes here as in all imperial residences — in doing nothing and in waiting that something may be done. I work a little, sketch from my window, and walk a great deal. There are but few persons at the Villa Eugénie, and all agreeable. Yesterday we took a charming walk along the Pyrénées, sufficiently near the mountains to see them in all their beauty and escaping the discomfort of constant ascents and descents. We lost our way and found only people who were ignorant of our fine French tongue: and this happens as soon as one quits the suburbs of Bayonne.

Yesterday the Prince Imperial gave a dinner party to a troupe of his young friends. The Emperor himself mixed the champagne with seltzer-water, but the effect was the same as if they had drunk the pure wine. They were all tipsy a quarter of an hour afterwards, and my ears still ache with the noise they made. I boldly undertook to translate a Spanish memoir respecting the site of Munda for His Majesty, which I begin to perceive is terribly difficult reading. I am working like a negro for my master, whom I shall go to see in a few days.

COMPIEGNE, *November*, 1861. — Our anticipated *fêtes* have been postponed by the death of His Majesty of Portugal. As lions we have four Highlanders in kilts, the Duke of Athol, Lord James Murray, with the son and nephew of the Duke.

It is droll enough to see these eight bare knees in a drawing-room where all the men are in knee breeches or pantaloons. Yesterday his Grace's piper was introduced, and they all four danced in a way to alarm the company when they whirled about. But there are some ladies here whose crinoline is still more alarming as they enter a carriage. As lady guests are not obliged to wear mourning, legs of every color are seen, the red stockings having a very good effect. In spite of walks through damp, icy woods, and red-hot drawing rooms, I have escaped a cold ; but I am oppressed and do not sleep.

I was present at the great ministerial comedy, where we were in expectation of several additional victims. The faces were a study, the speeches still more so ; inasmuch as M. Walewski, the tottering Excellency, paraded his griefs indiscriminately to friends and enemies. An inveterate prejudice is the strongest provocation to the utterance of nonsense, especially when one is in the habit of it. Oh human platitude ! His wife, on the contrary, was wonderfully cool and self-possessed. What is said of the Emperor's letter? He has a way peculiar to himself of saying things, and where he speaks as a Sovereign contrives to convey the impression that he is of a finer porcelain. I believe it to be precisely what is needed by our high-toned nation which has no love for common clay.

Yesterday the Princess of ——, when taking tea, asked a footman, in her German accent, "*De lui aborder ti sel bour le bain.*" After a quarter of an hour the man returned with thirty pounds of bay salt, supposing that she wished to take a salt bath.

A picture by Müller, representing Queen Marie Antoinette in prison, was lately brought to the Empress. The Prince Imperial asked who this lady was and why she was not in a palace. They explained to him that it was a Queen of France, and told him the meaning of a prison. He immediately ran off to ask the Emperor to be pleased to pardon this Queen whom he kept in prison. He is an odd child, and sometimes *terrible.* He says that he always bows to the people because they drove away Louis Philippe who was not on good terms with them. He is a charming child.

CANNES, *January*, 1862. — I have here as neighbor and companion M. Cousin, who has come to be cured of laryngitis, and who talks like a one-eyed magpie, eats like an ogre, and is surprised that he does not get well under this beautiful sky, which he sees for the first time. He is, moreover, very amusing, for he has the tact to draw out every one around him. I believe that when he is alone with his servant he talks with him as with the most coquettish Orleanist or Legitimist Duchess. The Cannites, *pur sang*, cannot get over their astonishment, and you may fancy, their look on being told that this man, who talks on every subject, and talks well, has translated Plato and is the lover of Madame de Longueville. The inconvenient part of it is that he does not know when to stop talking. For an eclectic philosopher it is a misfortune not to have adopted the conspicuous virtue of the sect of peripatetics.

How do you govern the little children who absorb you so much? It appears to be an interesting occupation. The worst thing about children is their tardy development which leaves us so long uncertain if they have mind or power of reasoning; it is vexatious that their struggling intelligence cannot be demonstrated by themselves. The main question is to know whether we shall talk sense or nonsense to them; each system has its pros and cons. I have made the acquaintance of a poor cat that lives in a cabin deep in the woods; I carry it bread and meat every day, and it runs a quarter of a league to meet me. I regret not being able to carry it off, for it has marvelous instincts.

LONDON, *British Museum*, *May*, 1862. — Frankly, the Exhibition is something of a failure. True, everything is not yet unpacked, but the building is horrible; although very large it does not impress one with its size, and one must walk and be lost in it to appreciate its extent. The English have made great progress in taste and the art of arrangement; we make furniture and painted paper assuredly better than than they, but we are in a deplorable path, and if this continue we shall be distanced. Our jury is presided over by a German who speaks English that is nearly incomprehensible, and nothing can be more absurd than our conferences ; no one even understands what subject is under discussion. Nevertheless, we vote. The worst of it is, that in our division there are some English manufacturers, and medals must necessarily be given to these gentlemen, who do not merit them. I am bombarded by speeches and routs. Two days ago I dined with Lord Granville. There were three small tables in a long gallery, which arrangement was expected to promote general conversation, but as the guests were but slightly known to each other nearly a general silence prevailed. In the evening I went to Lord Palmerston's, where the Japanese Embassy wore great swords which kept getting caught in all the women's dresses. I saw some women who were very beautiful and others who were very ugly ; both making a complete exhibition of their personal charms ; some attractive, others quite the reverse ; but each one displaying the same assurance.

LONDON, *June*, 1862. — I read my report yesterday to the International Jury, in the purest Anglo-Saxon, not a word drawn from the French. In vain do the Commissioners appeal and beat the drum, they cannot attract a crowd. Since the price has been reduced to a shilling fashionable people no longer go, and the lower class seem to find little pleasure in it. The restaurants are detestable, the American restaurant being the amusing feature, where may be found more or less diabolical beverages that one drinks through a straw : mint julep or "*raise the dead.*" All of these drinks are disguised gin. I am tired out with British hospitality and dinners which give the idea of all being prepared by the same inexpert cook. You cannot imagine how I long for a plate of soup from my own *pot-au-feu.*

I do not know which of two recent important events has produced the greatest effect, — one, the defeat of the two Derby favorites by an unknown horse ; the other, the defeat of the Tories in the House of Commons. The number of mournful faces in London was really ludicrous. A young married lady at the races fainted on learning that Marquis was beaten a head's length by a rustic without pedigree. Mr. Disraeli puts a better face on the matter and shows himself at every ball.

PARIS, *July*, 1862. — Madame de Montijo arrived last week, so changed that it is distressing to see her. Nothing consoles her for the death of her daughter, and I find her less resigned even than on the day of her death. I dined last week at Saint-Cloud with a small circle quite agreeably, and where the feeling struck me as being less papistic than is generally supposed. I was permitted to scandalize matters without being called to order. The little Prince is charming. He has grown two inches and is the prettiest child I have seen.

BAGNÈRES-DE-BIGORRE, *The Upper Pyrénées*, 1862. — I have arrived here with M. Panizzi after a little tour beneath a terrible sun, and find weather worthy of London: fogs and an imperceptible rain that penetrates to one's bones. The physician of this watering-place is an old comrade of mine who has auscultated me and punched my chest and back, discovering two mortal ailments of which he undertakes to cure me, provided that I drink daily two glasses from the hot mineral spring, which is not ill-tasting; and that I bathe in a warm spring that is very agreeable to the skin. Already I am better. There are not many persons here, the English and the grapes having failed this season. In point of beauty we have Mademoiselle A. D——, who formerly captivated Prince ——. I have only seen her back, and she wears the vastest crinoline to be found in all the country. Balls are given twice a week, which I shall not attend, and amateur concerts, which I shall religiously avoid. Yesterday I was compelled to undergo a musical mass, to which I was conducted by gensdarmes; but the *soirée* given by the Sub-Prefect I declined, not to accumulate too many catastrophes in a single day. I should like to show you the incomparable verdure of this region, to talk with you beneath the shade of the great beech-trees, and make you drink the bright water for which crystal would be no fitting comparison. The petty quarrels and occupations of which you complain are lamentably incidental to a provincial place, and one can only deplore the fate of persons condemned to live there. Nevertheless it is certain that in the course of a few months one sinks to the level of the natives, and becomes interested in provincial inanities. The confession is sad, but human intelligence accepts the aliment offered and with satisfaction.

Last week I made a mountain excursion to see a farm belonging to M. Fould. It is on the shore of a small lake, facing one of the finest panoramas imaginable, surrounded by great trees, a rare thing in France ; and one breakfasts there most capitally. He has many magnificent horses and oxen, the whole managed with English order.

Have you read "Les Misérables," and heard what is said of it ? This is another of the subjects in respect to which I find the human species below that of the gorilla. The world becomes more stupid every day.

BIARRITZ, *Villa Eugénie, September*, 1862. — Dear friend, I am here on the sea-shore, breathing more easily than for a long time. The waters of Bagnères made me ill, a proof, it was said, of their beneficial action ; but on leaving them I began to revive, and now the sea-air and perhaps also the superb *cuisine* have perfected my cure. There are but few guests at the Villa, and only amiable persons whom I have long known. There is no crowd in the town, not many French, the Spaniards and Americans predominating. At the Thursday receptions at the Villa the Northern and Southern Americans have to be placed on different sides of the *salon*, lest they should eat each other.

On these occasions there is full dress, but usually there is not the least toilette ; the ladies dine in high dresses, and we of the ugly sex in morning coats. There is not a château in France or England where one is so free and without etiquette, nor where the chatelaine is so good and so gracious to her guests. We take beautiful walks in the valleys skirting the

Pyrénées, returning with prodigious appetites. The lady bathers are, as usual, very odd in the matter of costume. There is a Madame ——, the color of a turnip, who arrays herself in blue and powders her hair, — the powder, however, is said to be ashes, with which she sprinkles her head because of her country's misfortunes.

Have you seen Victor Hugo's speech at a dinner of Belgian booksellers and other swindlers at Brussels? What a pity that this good fellow, who has such fine imagery at his command, should not possess an iota of common sense, nor the discretion to refrain from uttering platitudes unworthy of so clever a man! I find more poetry in his comparison of the tunnel and railway than I have met with in any book these five years. But they are, after all, merely metaphors, containing nothing of depth, solidity, or judgment. He is a man who intoxicates himself with his own words and does not take the trouble to think. The twentieth volume by Thiers pleases me, as it does you. I have read it a second time with renewed pleasure, and shall do so again. It was immensely difficult, in my opinion, to extract anything from the confused rubbish of the St. Helena conversations as reported by Las Cases, and Thiers has come out of it wonderfully well. I am also pleased with his comparison of Napoleon with other great men, although he is somewhat severe upon Alexander and Cæsar; nevertheless, there is much truth in what he says as to the absence of virtue on the part of Cæsar. It attracts great interest here, and I fear that there is not overmuch love for the hero; for instance, they will not concede the anecdote of Nicomedes, nor you either, I fancy. Adieu — keep well, and do not sacrifice yourself too much for others; they will come to accept it as a habit, and what is now a pleasure to you, will perhaps some day become an irksome duty.

PARIS, *October*, 1862. — I returned from Biarritz with my Sovereigns. We were all quite doleful, having been poisoned, as I believe, by verdigris. The cooks swear that they scoured their saucepans, but I do not credit their oaths. The fact is, fourteen persons at the Villa were seized with vomiting and cramps, and having formerly been poisoned with verdigris, I know the symptoms and hold to my opinion. What with the poisoning and the political stir, I have led an agitated life. I have been divided between the desire that M. Fould should remain in the Ministry, in the interest of our master, and the wish that he should resign for the sake of his own dignity and personal advantage. It has ended by concessions which have benefited no one, while, in my opinion, they have lowered the *dramatis personæ.* The joke of the matter is that Persigny, whom the non-papist Ministers cannot endure, has become their standard-bearer, and that he shall continue in office they have made the condition on which they retain their portfolios. So, Thouvenel, an intelligent, very good fellow, has been dismissed, while Persigny, who is crazy and understands nothing of business, remains. Here we are then, in the clutches of the clergy, and you know where they lead their friends.

I am now reading a book that may entertain you: the history of the "Revolt of the Netherlands," by Motley. There are not less than five thick volumes; but although not over and above well written, it is smooth in style and interesting. He yields too much to anti-Catholic and anti-Monarchical prejudice, but he has made immense researches, and though an American, is a man of talent.

I am suffering with my lungs. You will learn some day that I have ceased to breathe for want of this organ, which should induce you to be very amiable to me before this misfortune shall occur.

CANNES, *January,* 1863. — I have received the last novel by M. Gustave Flaubert, the author of "Madame Bovary," which I believe you have read, though you will not confess it. The new romance is "Salammbo," a crazy production; but the writer has talent which he fritters away under the pretext of realism. One obtains an amusing idea of the author, and a still more ludicrous one of his admirers, the *bourgeois,* who discuss such things with decent people. I recommend you to read a romance by M. de Tourguenieff, the proofs of which I am expecting for the "Revue des Deux Mondes," and which I have read in Russian. It is called "Les Pères et les Enfants." It offers a contrast between the passing and coming generation. The hero, the representative of the new generation, is a socialist, materialist, and realist, nevertheless a sensible and interesting man. This novel has produced a great sensation in Russia, and a great outcry against the writer, who is accused of immorality and impiety. When a work excites such public exasperation, it is, in my opinion, a signal proof of success.

Before leaving Paris I consulted an eminent physician, wishing to ascertain how long a time would be allowed to prepare for my funeral ceremonies. I was satisfied with the consultation, first, because the ceremony would not take place so soon as apprehended; secondly, because he explained clearly and anatomically the seat of my malady — not the heart, but the lungs. True, I can never be cured, but there are alleviations for my suffering. I have been in bed a week from an attack of spasms and suffocation, having contracted a painful lumbago, the effect of this fine climate, where, so long as the sun remains above the horizon one may fancy it to be summer; but as soon as it disappears we have a quarter of an hour of damp cold that penetrates to one's very marrow.

It appears that they are becoming more and more religious in Paris. I receive sermons from people from whom I should have expected something quite different. I am told that M de Persigny has shown himself ultra papist on the Senate's committee of address. I do not believe that there was ever a period when the world was more senseless (*bête*) than now. Last as long as it may, the end is ominous.

Paris, *April*, 1863. — Of all the Italian cities, Florence appears to me to have best preserved her characteristics of the Middle Ages. As to Rome let me give you two bits of advice: first, never to be a moment in the air at night-fall for fear of the Roman fever; but a quarter of an hour before the Angelus go to St. Peter's and wait until the strange, damp precipitate in the air shall pass by. There is nothing finer for meditation than this great church at that hour, the indistinctness of its vast proportions makes it truly sublime. Think of me when there. My second recommendation is to employ a rainy day in seeing the Catacombs. When there, turn into one of the narrow corridors debouching from the subterranean streets, extinguish your taper and remain alone for a few moments. You will tell me your sensations. I should have great pleasure in the experience with you, but perhaps our sensations would not be the same. I never succeeded in Rome in carrying out my programme of sight-seeing, for at each street corner one is drawn off by something unforeseen, and the great charm is to yield to impulse. As regards objects of art, study the frescoes, and the views as to nature and art combined. At the Capitol make them show you the wolf of the Republic, which bears trace of the thunderbolt that struck it in the time of Cicero. It is not a thing of yesterday. Try to understand that you cannot see the hundredth part of all that is interesting, and do not regret it; there will remain one great, harmonious memory worth more than a crowd of souvenirs in detail. Do not forget to see Pompey's statue, at the foot of which Cæsar was assassinated. Rome is pervaded with a gentle, agreeable melancholy which one recalls with pleasure; for a vivid comparison with which it would be well to pass a week at Naples. Of all transitions it is the most abrupt and amusing; it is comedy succeeding tragedy; and sends one to bed the mind filled with ludicrous images.

I do not know whether the *cuisine* has made any progress in the States of the Holy Father, but in my time it was the "abomination of desolation," while in Naples it was possible to subsist.

Society here is astir with the actual or reputed eccentricities of Madame de ——. Certain it is that she is crazy enough to be placed under restraint. She beats her servants, curfs, boxes the ears, and makes love to her favorites in the same breath. She carries her Anglo-mania so far as to drink brandy and water, that is to say, much of the former with little of the latter. The other evening she presented one of her friends to M. Troplong, saying: "*Monsieur le President*, I bring you my *darling*." To which M. Troplong politely replies, that he is happy to make the acquaintance of M. Darling. If all that is told me of the manners of the *liounes* be true, it is to be feared that the end of the world is near. I dare not tell you all that takes place in Paris among the young representatives of the generation that is to bury us.

CHÂTEAU DE FONTAINEBLEAU, *July*, 1863.—No one has time here for anything, and the days pass one knows not how. The chief occupation is eating, drinking, sleeping: I succeed in the first two, in the last very badly, after passing several hours in knee-breeches, in rowing on the lake and getting a frightful cough. There are many well assorted guests here, fewer officials than usual, which does not, however, detract from the prevailing *entente cordiale*. Sometimes we walk in the woods, after having picnicked on the grass like tradesmen from the Rue St. Denis.

Two days ago some very large chests arrived from his Majesty Tu-Duc, Emperor of Cochin China. They were opened in one of the court-yards. Within the large cases were smaller ones painted in red and gold, containing two very yellow elephant's teeth, two rhinoceros' horns, and a package of mouldy cinnamon, the whole exhaling inconceivable odors. There was also a large quantity of narrow gauze-like stuffs, of every ugly color, more or less soiled, and all musty. Medals, that were among the expected gifts, were absent, and probably remained in Cochin China; from which it appears that the great Tu-Duc is a swindler. Yesterday we attended the manœuvres of two regiments of cavalry, and were all cooked by the heat; all the ladies had a sun-stroke. To-day we are to have a Spanish dinner in the Forest, and I am intrusted with the *gaspacho*, that is to say, imposing raw onions on the ladies, who would swoon at the mere mention of the vegetable. I have forbidden that they be warned, and after they have eaten it, I shall make my confession to them in the style of Atreus.

LONDON, *August*, 1863.—I expected to find London empty, and in fact such was my first impression; but at the end of two days I discovered the great ant-hill to be still swarming, and, alas! that they dined quite as often and as interminably as last year. Is not the slowness of the dinners inhuman in this country! It really deprives me of appetite. We are never less than two hours and a half at table, and if the half hour during which the men leave the women to speak ill of them be added, it is always eleven o'clock when we return to the drawing-room. This would be but a demi-evil could one eat all the time; but, with the exception of the roast mutton, I find nothing to my taste.

The great men seem to me to have grown somewhat old since my last visit. Lord Palmerston has given up his false teeth, which changes him very much; but has preserved his whiskers, and has the air of a gay gorilla. Lord Russell looks less good-humored. The great beauties of the season have left town, but they are not very enthusiastically lauded. The toilettes, as usual, struck me as very inferior and crumpled; but nothing can resist this climate, of which my throat is also a proof. I am hoarse as a wolf, and suffer from suffocation. On my return to Paris, Panizzi will join me, and we are to be carried off to Biarritz by my gracious Sovereign Lady, who will lodge us for some time on the sea-shore.

Have you read Renan's "Life of Jesus?" It is the stroke of an axe to the edifice of Catholicism. The Bishop of Tulle has issued an order that all the nuns of his diocese shall recite *Aves* in M. Renan's honor, or rather to hinder the devil from flying off with everybody because of this same Renan's book. The author is so frightened at his own audacity in denying the Divinity, that he loses himself in hymns of admiration and adoration, to the disparagement of the philosophical intelligence by which alone the doctrine is to be judged.

Château de Compiègne, *November*, 1863. — Since my arrival here I have led the perturbed life of a manager, having been author, actor, and director. We have played with success a rather immoral piece, of which I will tell you the story on my return. We have had very fine fireworks, though a woman who examined the fusees too closely was killed outright. You do not tell me what has become of the charming child in whom you are interested. Train her, I beg of you, so that she be not a fool like the majority of women of the present day. If those in the Provinces are worse than in Paris, I do not know in what desert we shall seek refuge. We have here a fine slip of a girl, five feet four inches tall, with the pretty ways of a grisette, and a mixture of ease and honest timidity sometimes very amusing. Some fear was entertained lest the second part of a charade should not correspond with the beginning — (a beginning of which I was the author): "It will go off very well," said she: "We shall show our legs in the ballet, and that will make up for all." — N. B. Her legs are like flageolets and her feet are far from aristocratic.

Cannes, *January*, 1864. — I am charmed that Aristophanes is so fortunate as to please you. There are doubtless many things that shock your prudery, but which will interest you now that you have learned from Cicero something of ancient morals. You ask if the Athenian ladies attended the theatre. Learned men are divided in opinion on this point. It is probable that tolerance and intolerance prevailed at different periods in the same country, but it is certain that women never appeared on the stage, their *rôles* being enacted by men, which was the more easy from the custom of wearing masks during the performance. In Algeria you would have found, doubtless, women at the play. In the East, they have not now, and never had in ancient times, the prudery that prevails with women at the present day. An extraordinary point about Aristophanes is the unrestrained way in which he speaks of the gods, even on the occasion of their festival, for it was at the Dionysia that "The Frogs" was represented, in which

Bacchus plays so singular a part. The same thing took place in the first ages of Christianity. Comedies were played in church. There was the mass "des sots," and the mass "de l'Ane," the text of which still remains in a very curious manuscript. Apart from the nonsense that Aristophanes threw into his comedies as a seasoning of coarse salt, there are choruses of the finest poetry. My venerated master, M. Boissonade, was of opinion that no Greek had surpassed them. I recommend you to read "The Clouds," the masterpiece of Aristophanes. There is in it a dialogue between the Just and the Unjust, of the most elevated style. I think there is truth in his reproaches against Socrates; even after listening to him in Plato, one is tempted to forgive the hemlock. A man is a pest who, like Socrates, proves every one to be only a fool.

PARIS, *April*, 1864. — I rarely go into society, but I wished to pay my respects to my masters, whom I found in excellent health; which gave me also an opportunity of seeing the new fashions, which I admire but indifferently. It is a sign of old age. I cannot become accustomed to the mode of dressing the hair. Not a woman adopts the style suited to her own face; but all model themselves after the barber's blocks. One of my friends presented me to his wife, a young and pretty person, who was whitened, daubed with rouge, and her eyelashes painted. I was horrified.

Have you read About's book, "Le Progrès?" I do not know if it is successful, but it is very witty. Perhaps the clericals have had the good sense to withhold the excommunication that never fails to insure wide circulation to a work. It was their fulmination that secured Renan great pecuniary profit; his idyl having brought him one hundred and seven thousand francs. I keep subject to your order Taine's three thick volumes on the history of English Literature. The style is of a somewhat studied elegance, but very pleasant reading.

LONDON, *British Museum, July*, 1864. — From eight o'clock in the evening until midnight my life is passed at dinner parties, and the morning in looking at books and statues: or I work at my great article on the son of Peter the Great, which I am strongly inclined to entitle, "The Danger of being a Fool;" for the moral drawn from the work is that intellect is a necessity. You may find here and there something to interest you; notably, how Peter the Great — a detestable man and surrounded by detestable *canaille* — was deceived by his wife. I have carefully, and with some difficulty, translated his wife's love letters to her lover, who was impaled for his pains. These letters are really better than could be expected from the age and the country in which they were written; but love works wonders. The misfortune is that she knows nothing of orthography, thereby rendering her meaning somewhat obscure to a grammarian like myself.

Nothing is talked of here but the marriage of Lady Florence Paget, the beauty of London, the last two seasons. It would be impossible to find a prettier face on a more delicate figure, too slight and small for my special taste. She was noted for her flirtations. Mr. Ellice's nephew, Mr. Chaplin, of whom you have often heard me speak, a tall young fellow of twenty-five, and with twenty-five thousand pounds per annum, fell in love with her. She trifled with him a long time, finally became engaged to him, and, it is said, accepted from him jewels and six thousand pounds with which to pay her mantuamaker's bills. The wedding day was arranged, and last Friday they went together to the park and the opera. On Saturday morning she left home alone, and proceeding to St. George's Church was married to Lord Hastings, a young man of her own age, very ugly, and possessed of a slight fault — a passion for cards and wine. After the ceremony they started for the country, and at the first station she wrote to her father, the Marquis of Anglesey: "Dear Papa — As I knew you would never consent to my marriage with Lord Hastings, I was wedded to him to-day. I remain yours, etc." She also wrote to Mr. Chaplin: "Dear Harry — When you receive this I shall be the wife of Lord Hastings. Forget yours, very truly, Florence." Poor Mr. Chaplin, who is six feet high and has yellow hair, is in despair.

MADRID, *October*, 1864. — It is terribly cold and damp, and every one is ill, the bad weather having come upon us with excessive violence, according to the custom of this country, where gentle transitions, of whatsoever nature, are unknown. Imagine the misery of people who live on an elevated plateau exposed to every wind of heaven, their only stove being a *brasero*, a very primitive contrivance, giving one the choice of being frozen or asphyxiated. Civilization has made great progress here, but without a corresponding improvement. The women have adopted your absurd hats and wear them in the most uncouth fashion. The bulls are worthless, and the men who kill them are stupid and cowardly.

CANNES, *January*, 1865. — What do you think of the Pope's encyclical? I delight in reading the letters from the Bishops. There is a Bishop here, a man of wit and good sense, who veils his face. There are few attorneys more subtle than these gentlemen; but the most ingenious is M. D——, who makes the Pope say precisely the contrary of his encyclical and he may possibly be excommunicated at Rome. It is vexatious to serve in an army the General of which exposes one to defeat. Do they hope at Rome that the Marches, the Legations and the County of Avignon will be restored to them by a miracle? The misfortune is, that the world is so stupid that to escape the Jesuits it may be necessary to throw ourselves into the arms of mere blusterers.

The number of English here becomes more alarming every day. A hotel as large as that of the Louvre has been built on the sea-shore, which is always filled with these Islanders. One can no longer walk without meeting young Misses in Garibaldi *caracos* and hats with impossible feathers, making a pretense of sketching. There are croquet and archery parties of a hundred and twenty persons. I regret the good old times when one never met a soul.

Do you know that I received compliments from every quarter on my appointment as successor to M. Mocquard? I believed nothing of it, but by dint of seeing my name in the newspapers of various countries I began to be uneasy. With my disposition you may believe how well the position and I should agree!

Imagine my reading Lamartine's "Entretiens," in which I fell on a life of Aristotle, wherein he states that the retreat of the ten thousand took place after the death of Alexander. Would it not really be better worth while to sell steel pens at the gate of the Tuileries than to utter such enormities?

CANNES, *April*, 1865.—Your friend Paradol is Academician through the will of the burgraves, who for this purpose obliged the poor Duc de Broglie to return to Paris in spite of his gout and eighty years. It will be a curious sitting. Ampère once wrote a very bad history of Cæsar, and you may imagine all the allusions that M. Paradol will take occasion to make to this work, now forgotten by every one save the burgraves. Jules Janin remains outside of the door, as also my friend Autran from Marseilles, who, assuming the clerical, was abandoned by his religious friends.

You have heard, perhaps, that Mr. William Brougham, brother of Lord Brougham, and his successor in the peerage, has been caught in the fact in a very ugly matter of cheating. It causes great scandal here among the English colony. Old Lord Brougham puts a good face on it, and is, of course, a perfect stranger to all such villainy.

To teach myself patience, and to woo sleep, I am reading a book by Mr. Charles Lambert, who demolishes holy King David and the Bible. I find it very ingenious and rather amusing. Serious and pedantic books at which ten years ago no one would have dreamed of glancing, have now, thanks to the clergy, become popular and widely read. Renan has gone to Palestine to make new studies of landscape; Peyrat and this Charles Lambert are writing books still more serious and learned which sell like bread, my bookseller tells me.

LONDON, *British Museum*, *August*, 1865.—I have been here about six weeks, catching a few days of "the season," and have undergone some terrible dinners and two or three of the last routs. Lord Palmerston strikes me as having grown singularly old, notwithstanding the success of his elections, and it seems to me more than doubtful if he be equal to the approaching campaign. His retirement will insure a fine crisis. I have just passed three days with his probable successor, Mr. Gladstone, who did not amuse, but interested me, for I still find great pleasure in observing varieties of human nature, and here they are so different from our own as to excite an inexplicable wonder that within ten hours' distance bipeds without feathers should so little resemble those of Paris. In some respects Mr. Gladstone appears to me a man of genius, in others a child. There is in him something of the child, the statesman, and the *fou*. Five or six deans were at his house, and every morning the guests regaled themselves with a little prayer in common. I did not attend that of Sunday which must be something very curious. What surpassed everything was a sort of half-cooked roll that is taken hot from the oven for breakfast, the digestion of which gives one infinite trouble the rest of the day. In addition to this we had hard *civrn*, that is to say Welsh ale, which is very celebrated. You doubtless know that only red hair is worn. Nothing could be easier in this country, and I am quite sure it is not dyed. Not a single horse is to be seen in Rotten Row; but I rather like a great city in this state of semi-death. I profit by it to see the lions. Yesterday I passed an hour at the Crystal Palace watching a chimpanzee nearly as large as a child ten years old, and whom it so strongly resembled in its actions as to humiliate me by the incontestable relationship. I begin to tire of London, and thought for a moment of going to Scotland, but I should have fallen among sportsmen, a race I abhor.

PARIS, *September*, 1865. — I passed through Boulogne, which has improved both as to houses and inhabitants. I saw many fishwomen prettily dressed; but what Englishwomen, and what *pork pie* hats! These ladies should be warned that when lining the quay they make a great exhibition of their garters to steamer passengers coming in when the tide is low.

I am not dissatisfied with my article on "The History of Julius Cæsar." As the task was imposed on me, submission was unavoidable. You know how very highly I think both of the author and his book, and you also appreciate the difficulties besetting the critic who would deprecate the imputation of sycophancy and yet say nothing unbecoming, I have extricated myself pretty well, I hope. My text is, that the Republic had served its purpose, and that the Roman people were going headlong to the deuce when Cæsar stepped forth to save them. The thesis is true and easy to maintain, and I have merely written variations on that air.

I went yesterday to see Princess Murat, who has nearly recovered from her terrible accident, which she describes very graphically. She saw her coachman, a Swiss colonel, thrown high into the air, and four hours afterwards she found herself in bed, with her head the size of a pumpkin. During this interval she walked and talked, but she retains not the slightest remembrance of what passed from the moment of her fall. I hope, and it is probable, that in the moments preceding death there is also a loss of consciousness. I found Madame de Montijo recovering from the effect of her two operations. She extols highly her oculist Liebreich, who appears to be a great man.

PARIS, *October*, 1865. — Their Majesties have brought me back in a good state of preservation from Biarritz, where I passed my time as delightfully as possible. We had a visit from the King and Queen of Portugal. He is a timid German student; the Queen is charming, resembling the Princess Clotilde, but *en beau;* an improved edition. Her complexion is of that pure red and white, rare even in England; true, her hair is red, but of the very deep shade, now the fashion, and she is very affable and engaging in manner. They had with them a certain number of male and female caricatures, who were apparently collected for the occasion from some *rococo* shop. My good friend the Portuguese Minister led the Queen aside and made some complimentary remarks about me, which Her Majesty immediately repeated to me with much grace. The Emperor presented me to the King, who shook hands and looked at me with two great, round, astonished eyes that nearly made me fail in proper salutation to His Majesty. Another personage, M. de Bismarck, pleased me much more. He is a tall German, very polite and far from *naïf.* He is apparently utterly destitute of soul (*gemüth*), but all mind. He made a conquest of me. He brought with him a wife with the largest feet beyond the Rhine, and a daughter who walks in her mother's footsteps.

The Legitimists are in a nice state of uncertainty since the death of General Lamoricière ; and to-day I met an Orleanist of the old school who was equally disconsolate. How little it requires to be a great man now !

You cannot imagine the gossip caused by Princess Anna's marriage, nor the anger and comic rage of the Faubourg Saint-Germain. There was not a family having an unmarried daughter, who did not cherish designs against the Duke de Mouchy. The great question now agitating them is : "If they make visits shall we send them our cards ?" On the other hand there is now in Paris a young lady with several millions in her pocket, and some fifty more in expectancy. She is a very pretty and rather mysterious person, the adopted daughter of M. Heine, who died this year, and her origin is an enigma ; but on the strength of her millions the finest names of France, Germany, and Italy are ready for every absurdity. These adopted children are favorites of the goddess Fortune. The Greeks call them "children of the soul" —is it not pretty ? Have you read Victor Hugo's "Chansons des rues et des bois ?" Can you tell me if you perceive a difference between his former verses and those of to-day ? Has he suddenly become insane (*fou*), or has he always been so ? I incline to the latter view. We have only one man of genius remaining : M. Ponson du Terrail. Have you read his *feuilletons ?* No one else writes of crime and assassination with such skill as he exhibits. I quite revel in it. Were you here I should try to shake your orthodoxy in making you read a rather curious book on Moses, David, and St. Paul; not idyls after Renan, but dissertations somewhat too much interlarded with Greek, and even Hebrew. It is well worth reading, however, though the story of the Yankee, who, wishing to make a novel, makes a religion, and a flourishing religion, is only a stale invention.

CANNES, *January*, 1866. — How does it happen that with your taste for travelling, and having, moreover, the care of souls, you do not pass your winters at Pisa, or some other place where the great arbiter of human health is visible, Monsigneur the Sun? I am confident that but for him I should long since have been several feet under ground. All of my contemporaries are hastening to precede me. The past year has been severe upon a little circle of comrades who for several years have dined together once a month, and of which I am the sole survivor. This is the grave reproach that I address to the Great Mechanician — why do not men fall together, like the leaves of a season? Your Father Hyacinthe would not fail to utter some nonsense in reply: "O man, what are ten years, a century!" etc. What is eternity to me? The few days comprised in my span of life are of more importance to me. Why are they made so bitter?

You tell me nothing of Ponsard's piece, "Le Lion Amoureux." He has preserved the tradition of Corneille's verse rather emphatic, but grand, sonorous, and chaste. I imagine that people of society admire it as they admire M. Babinet's science, or the sermons of Abbé Lacordaire, the moment they were persuaded that it was genteel.

SAINT-CLOUD, *August*, 1866. — The Emperor has quite recovered from his illness, and has resumed his usual mode of life. It appears to me that everything tends to peace. It is very evident that M. de Bismarck is a great man, and so well prepared that it would be unwise to provoke his hostility

We shall have to swallow a few mortifications perhaps, and we shall continue to digest them until we are provided with needle-guns. It remains to be seen what the German parliament will do, and whether their advantages may not be lost by a few stupidities.

You asked me whence I derived my knowledge of the gypsy dialect: from M. Borrow, whose book is one of the most curious that I ever read. What he relates of the gypsies is perfectly true, and his personal observations agree perfectly with my own, except on one point. In his character of clergyman he was naturally deceived in matters respecting which I, as a Frenchman and *laic*, have a clearer insight from personal experience. It is exceedingly singular, however, that this man, gifted in languages to the extent of speaking the Cali dialect, should possess so little grammatical perspicacity as not to see at a glance that many words unknown in Spanish have remained in this dialect. He asserts that only the roots of Sanskrit words have been preserved.

BIARRITZ, *September*, 1866.—Four days of the week we have rain, the remainder being suffocatingly warm, accompanied by a horrible sirocco; but the sea is much finer here than at Boulogne, and figs and ortolans aid us in sustaining the burden of life. The other day we made a charming mountain excursion to see two famous grottoes on the Spanish border, in one of which we found twenty contrabandists, who sang Basque choruses, accompanied by a little sharp flageolet that has a very wild and agreeable effect. The music is full of character, but sad, like all music of mountaineers. As to the words, I only understood "*Viva Emperatriça.*" Our guide was a singular man, who had made a large fortune by smuggling. He is the king of these mountains; every one obeys his orders. While we followed the open paths with difficulty, it was fine to see him galloping among the rocks, clearing all obstacles, calling to his men in French, Spanish, and Basque; never making a false step. The Empress commissioned him to watch over the Prince Imperial, whom, on his pony, he led through almost impassable roads, having as much care of him as of a bale of contraband merchandise. We stopped an hour at his house at San, where we were received by his daughters, who are well educated, well dressed and not at all provincial, differing only from Parisians in the pronunciation of *r*, which with the Basques is always *r-r-r-h*.

PARIS, 1866. — While at Biarritz a discussion arose one day as to the perplexing situations in which one might be placed, as for example, Rodrigo between his papa and Chimene, or Mademoiselle Camille between her brother and her Curatius. The same night, having taken some over strong tea, I wrote fifteen pages, depicting a situation of this kind. The story is perfectly moral *au fond*, but there are details of which Monseigneur Dupanloup might disapprove. It is not, I think, the worst thing I ever wrote, although written very hastily. I read it to the lady of the house (the Empress). There was then at Biarritz the Grand Duchess Marie, daughter of Nicholas, to whom I had been presented some years previously. Shortly after the reading I was visited by a policeman, announcing himself sent by the Grand Duchess. "What is your pleasure?" "I come on the part of her Imperial Highness to beg you to wait on her this evening with your romance." "What romance?" "That which you read the other day to Her Majesty." I replied that I was Her Majesty's jester, and that I could not work elsewhere without her leave; and straightway I hurried to tell the Empress what had passed. I expected that it would at least result in a war with Russia, and was not a little mortified at being not only authorized, but entreated to go in the evening to the Grand Duchess, to whom the policeman had been assigned as a factotum. Nevertheless, to console myself I wrote a letter to the Grand Duchess in rather strong terms, and announced my visit to her. On the way with the letter to her hotel, I met in a little side-street a woman, who, the wind being high, was in danger of being blown into the sea, her petticoats having been caught up by the wind, and who, blind and giddy with the noise of the crinoline, and the dread of the possible consequences, was quite overwhelmed with embarrassment. I ran to her assistance, had much difficulty in aiding her effectually, and then only did I recognize the Grand Duchess. The gust of wind spared her some little epigrams. Besides, she showed herself a very good Princess to me, and gave me excellent tea and cigarettes; for, like almost all the Russian ladies, she smokes. Her son, the Duke of Leuchtenberg, is a very fine fellow, with a good air, is amiable, reads Schopenhauer, holds to the positive philosophy, is a little of a Republican and Socialist, and a nihilist into the bargain, like Tourguenieff's Bazarof; for princes in the present age do not think that the Republic progresses with sufficient rapidity.

July, 1867.—I have not been dazzled by the Exposition. I saw some fine Chinese objects too dear for my purse. Some Russian carpets, already sold. You appear enchanted with the bazaar, and if you will some morning be my guide there, your enthusiasm may awaken mine. The Japanese pleased me very much. Their skin, the color of *café-au-lait*, is of an agreeable tint; but as well as I could judge from the folds of their robes, their limbs are as small as the slats of chairs, which is a pity. As I noted the crowd of loungers surrounding them, I could but think that Europeans would have less self-possession in presence of a Japanese public. Imagine yourself, *you*, being exhibited at Yeddo, and a grocer saying: "I should like to know if the hump this lady wears beneath her dress is really a part of herself!" Come soon and give me your opinion about the Sultan and the Princes who had the privilege of looking at you for three hours. Would it not have been better to bring me the bouquet yourself? You pained me by sending it.

I fear that this shooting of Maximilian will ruin our affairs, which were proceeding satisfactorily. It is a sad pity.

The Pacha of Egypt has made two visits to Mademoiselle ——, which I dare not relate to you, although they were very curious. He has been reconciled to his cousin Mustapha, but they have not yet been induced to take coffee together, each one being persuaded, in view of the progress in chemistry, that it would be dangerous.

Something beautiful was lately brought to me ; a shield with *fleur-de-lis*, setting a miniature portrait of Marie Antoinette, probably made at Vienna before her marriage, and given to the Princess de Lamballe. The back had contained hair, now lost. After some resistance I allowed myself to be conquered, and purchasing it sent it at once to Her Majesty who is making a collection of everything that ever belonged to Marie Antoinette. It will certainly be one of the prettiest souvenirs, is undoubtedly authentic, and was long worn by Madame de Lamballe. For myself I have a horror of these sad antiquities, but one cannot dispute tastes.

PARIS, *October*, 1867.—You speak, dear friend, of a vegetable life, which in truth one would prefer to lead in this age ; but the world moves, and human vegetables are as unfortunate as those who live at the foot of Etna ; from time to time a stream of fire descends on them, and nearly always they are enshrouded by sulphurous vapor. Is it not deplorable that Pius IX. and Garibaldi, two fanatics, should throw everything into disorder through their obstinacy ? One thing that demonstrates the morals of the present day, is, that the persons who blame the sending of our troops to Rome, say, when reminded of the treaty of September : " What matters a treaty ? M. de Bismarck does not adhere to them ! " I am inclined to steal their watch and tell them that precedents for stealing watches may be found. The most distressing point in all this is, that we have renewed our pledge, for how long a time I do not know, to protect the Pope, who does not feel the slightest gratitude. All that is said for and against the temporal power is so silly, so absurd, that I blush for my century. Another subject that makes me furious is the project for the reorganization of the army. All the well-born young men are dying with fright at the notion of fighting for their country at any given moment, and say that this vulgar method must be left to the

Prussians. Imagine for a moment what will remain to the French nation should she lose her military courage!

I am still suffering, breathing with difficulty, and on the eve of breathing no longer. M. Fould's sudden death has grieved me very much; it was the serenest that could be wished; but why so quick? He wrote eighteen letters the morning of his death, and had previously seemed perfectly well. He had apparently not moved in bed, and no contraction of his features was observable. It is just such a death as was that of Mr. Ellice, and is what the English call "visitation of God."

CANNES, *December*, 1867. — I am uncertain how long I may be able to remain here; it depends on the Pope, Garibaldi, and M. de Bismarck; I, like the rest of the world, being somewhat in the hands of these gentlemen. I am really alarmed by the political situation, and in the general tone of the press and public speakers find a reminder of 1848 — strange and angry agitation without apparent cause. The nerves of all are on the stretch. M. Thiers, after passing his entire life in political conflict, is seized with nervous trembling because a Marseilles lawyer utters platitudes that only deserve to be smiled at. Most vexatious of all is this M. Rouher, who wishes to out-Herod Herod, and uses expressions the reverse of politic, from which every Minister should abstain.

I know of nothing more shameful than Garibaldi's conduct; if ever a man was under obligation to kill himself, assuredly it was he. To go off to Caprera after causing the death of some hundreds of simpletons, appears to me the height of disgrace for the revolutionists and the English noblemen who thought this animal something other than a dancing jack. It is annoying, also, that the Pope is thoroughly convinced that he owes nothing to us, and that it is Heaven that has done all for love of his *beaux yeux*.

What shall I say to you of the policy of M. Ollivier and *tutti quanti?* In vain do they turn elegant phrases and affirm that they are thoroughly satisfied; they seem to me merely second-rate actors, who play the first *rôles* in a manner that can deceive nobody. We are daily becoming smaller. The only truly great man is M. de Bismarck.

A propos, might it be true that he spent the secret-service money? I consider the purchase of the journals very probable; but as M. de Bismarck will not send his receipts to M. de Kerveguen, I suppose that these gentlemen will come off with honor.

CANNES, *February*, 1868.— I am sometimes the greater part of the day unable to breathe; not a sharp pain but a teasing discomfort that acts on the nerves. I am more and more melancholy, and yield to gloomy forebodings. I do not succeed in accustoming myself to suffer, and am irritated by it, which only adds to the evil. I am reading an over-long and badly written book, the author of which, however, appears to be honest, and relates what he has seen and heard: it is Dixon's "New America." His reflections must be passed by, for he is somewhat silly. He saw the Mormons, and what is even more curious, the republic of Mount Lebanon; that and Fenianism give an idea of America which Talleyrand's *mot* defines precisely.

I am delighted that my article on Pouchkine should not have wearied you. I have not the works with me, and the verses quoted are those that I learned by heart during the time of my great Russian enthusiasm. There are many Russians here, and I commissioned a friend to procure me the volume of Pouchkine's detached poems if it could be found in the Muscovite colony here. He made inquiry of a very pretty woman, who, in place of the verses, sent me a huge bit of fish from the Volga, and two birds from the same region, all cooked within a few metres of the North pole. They were pretty good. The fish must be a fine fellow of some five or six feet, to judge from my specimen slice. This lady, Madame Voronine, has a charming head, her husband the unmistakable look of a Calmack. The lady at first refused him her hand. He put a pistol to his head, missed fire, and for his pains she married him. As for the Englishmen and Englishwomen, never has there been so great a number with impossible hair and toilettes, red stockings, parasols, and paletots lined with grebe skin. Among other extraordinary Englishmen there is the Duke of Buccleugh, who has a horn in the middle of his forehead, and his son inherits the peculiarity. It projects from the skull, and will end I fear in playing them an ill turn.

The discussion on the press disgusts me. Every one lies too much, and not an idea is suggested that has not already been twenty times expressed in better terms. It strikes me that the level of intelligence is greatly lowered, as well as that of honesty. It is all very sad. I saw yesterday a friend just returned from Montana, who tells me that the Garibaldians were well whipped, and that they were a singular mixture of vile rabble and the flower of aristocracy.

MONTPELLIER, *April*, 1868. — Dear friend, I suffered so intensely before coming here as to lose all courage; it was impossible to think, still more so to write. Chance brought to my knowledge a physician of this place who treats asthma by a new method, and since my trial of it during the last five days, my condition seems to be ameliorated, and the physician gives me hope. Every morning I am placed in a great iron cylinder that resembles, I confess, one of the monuments erected by M. de Rambuteau. There is an arm-chair within, and glazed apertures give sufficient light by which to read. The door is closed, the air of the cylinder is compressed by means of a steam-engine, producing the sensation of needles penetrating the ear, to which one becomes accustomed after a few seconds, and what is of more importance, one begins to breathe with wonderful ease. At the end of half an hour I fell asleep. The physician, who has nothing of the charlatan about him, thinks my case by no means desperate.

Have you read Abbé Dupanloup's letter? The soul of Torquemada has entered his body, and he will burn us all if we do not take care. I fear that the Senate will do, and say everything calculated to make itself ridiculous and odious. You would not believe what terror these old generals, who have already passed through so many perilous adventures, now have of the devil. I do not know whether Sainte-Beuve is in a condition to speak, as the journals state; I doubt it, and moreover am by no means certain if he would deal with the question in the best way; I mean to ward off this bombshell. His duty is to speak his mind boldly, regardless of consequences, as he did on the subject of Renan's book. All this irritates and torments me.

CHÂTEAU DE FONTAINEBLEAU, *August*, 1868.—I have been here a fortnight finding idleness to be a good thing for body and soul. The trees and sky are a perpetual delight. There are not more than thirty persons at the château, the only ones not in waiting, besides myself, being some amiable cousins of the Empress; gentlemen and ladies whom I knew at Madrid. I have made a copy of a portrait of Diana of Poitiers after Primatice; she is represented as Diana with her quiver, and she undoubtedly sat for the picture. as from the head to the feet it is evidently a likeness. Moreover, if I may dare to say it, the examination of the legs proves that she gartered below the knee according to the fashion of the time, which is now abandoned, as I hear. I will show it to you, as it is a portrait of historical importance.

I dined yesterday with Sainte-Beuve who interested me exceedingly. Although he still suffers he has charming wit, and is assuredly one of the most agreeable talkers whom I have ever conversed with. He is greatly alarmed by the progress of the clericals, and takes the matter to heart. I believe that the danger does not lie on that side.

So poor Rossini is dead. His friends say that he continued to work, although not wishing to publish the result of his labor; but that appears to me highly improbable; for the immense value that he placed on money would have induced him to publish. He was one of the most *spirituel* men I have ever known, and nothing more marvelous has been heard than the song of Figaro, from the "Barber of Seville," as sung by himself. No actor was comparable to him. The past year has been fatal to great men. Lamartine and Berryer are said to be dangerously ill.

CANNES, *February*, 1869. — I am sad and suffering, not the least amendment! On the contrary the doctors have not even succeeded in alleviating the painful spasms that seize me from time to time. We have a magnificent sea and sky, and these influences that formerly restored me to health no longer avail. What must be done? I only know that my desire for the end is unceasing.

I have been reading with much interest "The Memoirs of a Scotch Peasant," who by dint of intelligence and labor became a man of letters, a professor of geology and a person of celebrity. Unfortunately he cut his throat a short time ago, overwork having, without doubt, entirely worn out his brain. His name is Hugh Miller. It seems to me that everything is going to ruin. There is no longer a Spain, soon there will be no Holy See. The loss will be more or less great according to men's ideas.

PARIS, *June*, 1869. — The disturbances that are of nightly occurrence on the Boulevards, and which recall the fine days of 1848, contribute not a little to sadden me, and I exclaim with Hamlet: "Man delights me not, nor woman either." What most afflicts me in these disheartening affairs is the profound stupidity. This nation, who believes and styles itself the most *spirituel* on earth, testifies its desire to enjoy Republican government by demolishing the booths where poor people sell newspapers. It cries "*Vive la Lanterne!*" and it breaks street lamps. It makes one hide one's face. The danger is that there is a sort of emulation for stupidity as for everything else, and between the Chambers and the Government, God only knows what may be done!

I pass my time in deciphering letters of the Duke d'Albe and Philip II., given to me by the Empress. They both wrote like cats. I begin to read Philip quite fluently, but his general still perplexes me. I have just read one from him addressed to his august master, written a few days after the death of Count Egmont, in which he is moved to pity by the fate of the Countess, who has not a morsel of bread after having had a dowry of ten thousand florins. Philip says the simplest things in an involved, long-drawn style ; it is very difficult to guess his meaning, and it seems to be his constant aim to confuse his reader and force him to take the initiative. They were certainly the most odious couple of men who ever existed, and unfortunately neither was hung, which is not to the praise of Providence. I have also received a very curious book from England, in which it is claimed that Jeanne la Folle was not crazy, but a heretic, for which reason mamma, papa, her husband and son came to a clever agreement to keep her in prison, with, from time to time, a little torture.

PARIS, *June*, 1869. — I am reading Renan's "Saint Paul" with difficulty. Decidedly, he has a monomania for landscape ; and instead of keeping to his text he describes the woods and fields. Were I an *Abbé* I should amuse myself by writing a review of it. Have you read the harangue of our Holy Father the Pope ? I am quite sure that we are about to have in words and deeds enormities for which there will not be enough roasted apples. Alas ! things may end in still harder projectiles. What a misfortune that the modern mind should be so vapid ! Do you believe that it was ever before so much so ? Doubtless there have been ages when people were more ignorant, more barbarous, more absurd ; but there were here and there some great geniuses as a compensation ; whilst now, it seems to me, there is a universal depreciation of intellect.

Some one has sent me Baudelaire's works, which have infuriated me. Baudelaire was insane ! He died in the hospital after writing verses that gained him Victor Hugo's esteem, and which had no other merit than that of being prejudicial to morals. Now he is regarded as an unappreciated man of genius !

PARIS, *August*, 1869. — I passed a month at Saint-Cloud in tolerable health, the open air renewing my strength, but on my return was seized with distressing oppression, when my physician from Cannes arrived with a newly discovered remedy of his own that relieved me; this was eucalyptus pills, the eucalyptus being an Australian tree naturalized at Cannes.

At Saint-Cloud, by command of the Empress, I read "The Bear," now called "Lokis," meaning bear in *jmoude*, before a very select audience, including several young ladies, who appeared to see no harm in it; this has encouraged me to make a present of it to the "Review," since it causes no scandal. Tell me exactly what you think on the subject, holding the balance even as to the *pour et contre*. The progress in hypocrisy during this age must be taken into consideration. What will your friends say?

A few days ago I dined with the innocent Isabella, and found her superior to my anticipations. Her husband, who is very small, is a polished gentleman, and paid me many well-turned compliments. The Prince of the Asturias is a very nice lad, with an air of intelligence. He resembles ——, and the infantas of the time of Velasquez.

The Emperor's illness is not serious, but it may be prolonged and there may even be a relapse.

I design writing a life of Cervantes to serve as preface to a new translation of "Don Quixotte." Is it long since you have read it, and does it still amuse you? I find it entertaining, for which I can give no valid reason; on the contrary, I could offer many that would prove the book to be bad; nevertheless, it is excellent.

CANNES, *November*, 1869. — I breakfasted yesterday at Nice with M. Thiers, who is much changed physically since the death of Madame Dosne, but not at all so morally, it seemed to me. His mother-in-law was the soul of his house; she drew people to his *salon*, and understood how to make it attractive to politicians and others. In short, she was queen of a court composed of very heterogeneous elements, which she had the art of turning to the profit of M. Thiers. Now, solitude has begun for him; his wife will interest herself about nothing. In politics I found M. Thiers still more changed; he has regained his senses in perceiving how extreme the folly with which the country is possessed, and is ready to combat it again as in 1849. I fear that he deludes himself somewhat as to his strength. It is much easier to burst the bags of Æolus than to mend and make them air-tight. It seems probable that we are coming to a fight; the *chassepot* is omnipotent and can give the populace a historic lesson, as General Changarnier said; but will it be used to good purpose? Personal government has become impossible, and parliamentary government without good faith, without honesty, and without men of sagacity, seems to me no less impossible. In short, the future, and I might say the present, looks very dark to me.

CANNES, *January*, 1870. — To-day I am suffering less, and avail myself of the respite to write to you. I am much discouraged; I have tried every remedy, but the suffering still returns with such intensity as almost to banish sleep. I not only do not eat but have a horror of all nutriment. I can hardly read, and often cannot discern what is before my eyes. Such, dear friend, is my situation. I am certain that it is a slow and very painful death that is approaching. I must make up my mind to it.

Politics, which I no longer understand, offer no agreeable distraction. It appears to me that we are striding towards a worse revolution than the one that we passed through so gayly twenty years ago. I should be glad were the performance a little delayed, that I might not be a spectator.

So you have had a disturbance as stupid as its instigator (Victor Noir). We offer but a sad spectacle in our abuse of liberty and parliamentary government. It is impossible not to be struck with the truly laughable audacity with which, in the Chamber, the most monstrous *spropositi* which no one would venture to enunciate in a drawing-room are presented and supported. This representative *régime* is hardly an amusing comedy; every one in it lies shamelessly, and yet allows himself to be caught by the most plausible speaker. There are even people who believe Cremieux to be eloquent, and Rochefort a great citizen. People were stupid in 1848, but they are infinitely more so now.

CANNES, *May*, 1870. — My health is irretrievably destroyed. I cannot yet accustom myself to this life of suffering and privation ; but whether resigned or not I am a doomed man. Wishing to make an experiment and ascertain if I could bear the journey to Paris, I lately went to Nice to pay some visits. I thought for a moment that I should commit the indiscretion of dying at the house of some one with whom I was not sufficiently intimate to take that liberty. I envy some of my friends who have contrived to leave this world suddenly, without suffering and without the tedious warnings that reach me daily. The political commotion of which you speak has also invaded this petty corner of the world. I have seen here very clearly how stupid and ignorant the men are. I am convinced that very few of the electors have understood what they were doing. The Reds, who here are in the majority, have persuaded the imbeciles, still more numerous, that there was a project to impose a new tax. The result is good. (The vote for the plebiscite.) "It is well cut, the question now is to sew it up," as Catherine de Medicis said to Henri III. Unfortunately, I know few persons in this country who are skillful with the needle. What think you of my friend M. Thiers, who, after the history of the banquets of 1848, begins anew the same tactics ? It is said that magpies are never caught twice in succession by the same trap ; but men, and clever men, are much more easy to ensnare.

PARIS, *July*, 1870. — One must be in vigorous health and possess nerves of exceptional strength not to be affected by the events now crowding about us. There is no need to explain to you all that I feel on this subject. I am of those who believe that this thing could not be avoided (the war with Prussia). The explosion might have been retarded, but to exorcise the animus of it was impossible. Here, the war is more popular than it has ever been, even among the *bourgeois.* They brawl loudly, 't is true, a bad thing ; but they enlist and give money, which is the one essential. The military are full of confidence ; but when we remember that the whole future is at the mercy of a bullet or a ball, it is difficult to share their trust.

PARIS, *August*, 1870. — It would not be well for you to come to Paris just now. I fear that in a short time only sad scenes would greet you. Only men given up to dejection, and drunkards shouting the Marseillaise are seen. Great disorder everywhere. The army deserves all praise, but it appears that we have no generals. All may yet be retrieved, but for this a miracle must supervene. I am not more ill, only overwhelmed by the situation. I write from the Senate, where we do little save exchange hopes and fears.

PARIS, *August*, 1870. — Affairs seem to assume a somewhat brighter aspect these few days past, yet I see everything *en noir.* The military are sanguine. The soldiers and the *Gardes Mobiles* fight bravely, and it appears that Marshal Bazaine's army has accomplished prodigies although always opposed one to three. Now, to-morrow, to-day perhaps, we may expect another great battle. The late actions have been appalling. The Prussians make war by massing men (*coups d'hommes*), and until now this method has been a success ; but it seems that the carnage around Metz was such as to give them food for thought. It is said that the young ladies of Berlin have lost all their waltzers. If we could reconduct them to the frontier, or bury them here, which would be better, even then we should not be at the end of our calamities. This horrible butchery, it is useless to dissemble, is only the prologue to a tragedy of which only the devil knows the *dénoûement.* A nation is not shaken as ours has been with impunity. A revolution must follow, whether we are victorious or defeated. All the blood that has flowed or that shall flow, will inure to the profit of the Republic — that is to say, to organized disorder.

Adieu, dear friend. Remain at P——, where you are safe. We are still quiet here ; we await the Prussians with much cool ness, but the devil will not be the loser. Once more — Adieu.

CANNES, *September* 23, 1870.[1] — Dear friend, I am very ill, so ill that writing is a difficult matter. There is a slight improvement. I will write to you soon, I hope, more in detail. Send to my house at Paris for the "Letters of Madame de Sévigné" and "Shakespeare." I ought to have sent them to you before my departure. Adieu. *Je vous embrasse.*

[1] The last letter — written two hours before his death.

TWENTY-FIVE YEARS OF MY LIFE.

BY

ALPHONSE DE LAMARTINE.

TRANSLATED BY LADY HERBERT.

TWENTY-FIVE YEARS OF MY LIFE

BOOK I.

I.

AS to the interest which these memoirs will have in a literary or political sense, I do not exaggerate it one way or the other; but the following are the reasons which make me think I shall at least be forgiven for their publication.

I was born in the very midst of the French Revolution — a time of passion, folly, and fury of parties on all sides. My first recollections are of a father in prison; of a mother a captive on parole in her own house, under a revolutionary guard; of the songs of the "Marseillaise" and the "Ça ira," sung in the streets, and echoing, as it were, the anguish in the bosom of the families around us; of the dull *thuds* which followed the stroke of the guillotine in our public squares; of the march of half-scared troops all day long on the highway. I used to sing myself the songs I heard others sing — poor, little, unintelligent echo that I was of a world into which I had just entered amidst smiles and tears! My poor mother used to look at me sadly enough. One day a change came: the soldiers overpowered the demagogues; the guillotine was swept away, and my own family could breathe freely again. We went to seek a humble shelter among our faithful peasants in the country. Little by little we obtained the kind of security granted to proscribed persons. Year after year my sisters came to brighten the home, which our devoted servants always maintained on the most comfortable footing; and here I grew and throve in the midst of our people.

My mother taught me the existence of that mysterious and Divine Being who is Justice, Power, and what we call Providence. This was to me a great joy: my little mind had been always working; now I had found a key to the problem of life — the only real and true foundation — in a word, I believed, and prayed. My heart opened to these pious influences; the spirit of a man began to develop itself in me; in a word, the child was being matured. Then came my school and college life, when rude hands fashioned me, in sad contrast to the gentle, loving training of my home. I passed through this ordeal, and came out of it transformed but not improved. I was an excitable lad, like a will-o'-the-wisp, with no very fixed ideas, and willing enough to float down the flowery stream of life. The Revolution broke out again, and I looked upon it as solving for me the mystery of the future. I went into the army: I loved the Bourbons, and thought I would die to serve them. But when peace came I was soon sick of a military life. Napoleon returned, and there was an end of my dreams of glory. I accompanied the Bourbon princes to the frontiers of France, but I did not go beyond — I felt that I belonged to my country above all else. Then came the bloody field of Waterloo: the 20th of March was avenged, and the Bourbons were reinstated. I again took my place in their guard, both from a feeling of honor and of fidelity. But I did not remain there long: I could not stand a life of inactivity and of discipline without glory; so I again became a vagabond and a wanderer on the face of the earth. Travelling not only dispels our *ennui*, but interests and fills the heart. I led a life of pleasure and of love for several years; then followed sadness, dissatisfaction, and remorse. I resolved at last to do something, and went into diplomacy, for which I felt I was well qualified. Not long after I married a good and accomplished woman, who brought me back to all virtuous and domestic habits, and I became once more satisfied, calm, and happy.

The Revolution of 1830, which drove the elder branch of the Bourbons into exile, induced me to share their fate, in spite of the wishes of the Orleans princes, whom I was very willing to respect, but whom I could not serve. I started for the East, and for two years diverted my mind by travelling in Turkey, the Archipelago, the Holy Land, Syria, and the Lebanon. I came home. My reputation had grown during my absence. I found myself elected a member of the Senate. I resolved to abstain from party votes or passions, and to devote myself entirely to the good of my country; thus giving up any chance of promotion or public employment, but preserving my own principles and self-respect. I conquered at last a certain position for myself, but with difficulty. Certain literary successes at this time added slightly to my reputation. After ten years, party strife and passions got the upper hand. The very men who had brought about the Revolution of 1830, and the Government of the Orleanists, turned against their own work. I opposed them vigorously; but I refused everything save the pleasure of defeating and overthrowing them. I could not bear that my indignation should be attributed to any other feeling than one of right. I repudiated all idea of intrigues and revolutionary banquets. I struggled at one and the same time against the coalition and the royalists of 1830. I had the happiness of being understood by the country and the King, who sent for me and begged me to take office. I refused, though with respectful firmness. I chose to have no *rôle* but that of a volunteer: all for my country, nothing for myself. The crisis became imminent: there were risings in various places; the Ministers lost their heads; the coalition disbanded itself; the King lost his presence of mind; the people were in a ferment. At last the Revolution, with which I had nothing on earth to do, was declared. I was only mixed up in it during the last few hours, after the flight of the King. I appeared like Fate, to repress, and, if possible, keep it within bounds. It has been said and written that such and such a faction or secret society brought it about. This is not true. I can appeal to the ocular testimony of thousands—not in defence of myself, but to bear witness to the fact that, finding the Revolution inevitable, it was I who organized it; and unless we had been content with utter anarchy, what else was there to be done? I asked it of the whole of France. It was a bold step; but it was a necessary one. The alternative was only a continued and aggravated anarchy. *Felix culpa!* The Republic once proclaimed, I found the means of moderating its action. France behaved admirably. For four months we governed in the midst of the storm, without what one may call a government at all. Afterwards everything was changed. I refused what was offered to me, and returned into obscurity. I had not the vanity to pretend to that to which neither my birth nor my talents entitled me. I bore without complaint fifteen years of unjust reproaches and of continued misfortunes, under which I am now sinking. I worked on courageously, however: I am working still. These events may interest my readers—I write them in good faith. May God be my helper!

II.

I was born at Mâcon, a pretty little town of Lower Burgundy, in 1790. My grandfather was a man of high rank. He was a fine-looking old man, but one who cared for nothing but the pleasures of society. He had served for a long time in the cavalry during his youth—without, however, rising above the rank of captain—which was the custom among the gentry of the provinces in those days. He was very rich. His principal estates were in Burgundy, and in the neighborhood of Mâcon; but he had also property at Péronne, Champagne, Monceau, Milly, and Ursy, near Dijon. In Franche-Comté, which was the home of his wife, he had also a beautiful estate, near St. Claude; the Forest of Fresnoy, of which the wood would now be worth many millions, but of which I witnessed the sale as a boy for about 60,000 francs to an old farmer, out of sheer disgust at having a few leagues to go for its superintendence; also a property at Villars, which he gave to one of my aunts ; that of Amorandes, with the ruins of a fine old castle ; that of Poligny ; and last, not least, the valuable manufactories of Morez, which had been begun and worked by himself. He rarely went to visit his outlying properties. His usual home was the Château of Monceau, near Mâcon, of the origin of which I know nothing, but which I have a good deal enlarged, and which is still in my possession. Monceau was then a fine country-house on the road to Cluny, with imposing looking gardens, terraces, and lawns on the one side, and on the other a quantity of outbuildings and vineyards, with the houses of the vinedressers and laborers, which gave it the stamp of opulence and plenty. In the midst of all my debts and difficulties, I jealously guard this last remains of the fortune of my ancestors, so that I may at least die where my fathers have died. In my grandfather's time there were at Monceau large vineyards, fine houses, extensive silkworm plantations, a pretty theatre, plenty of visitors, and stables full of horses for the owner and his visitors. It was his favorite summer residence. The views on all sides are magnificent. After passing through a long avenue, bordered with rich vineyards, the eye follows the road, which opens into a beautiful and fertile valley, the blue smoke from the shepherds' houses rising here and there among the trees, and adding to the beauty of the view.

After being set at liberty, my grandfather never went back to Monceau. Age and heavy cares induced him to remain with his wife and children in his town-house at Mâcon : everything around him had become sad. In the evening some old friends or relations, and one or two proscribed priests, would steal through the badly-lighted corridors, and take their places almost silently at the whist table ; for the Revolution had not interrupted the nightly rubber. But they played secretly ; and when the game was over, they lighted their little paper lanterns and disappeared through the narrow streets of the old town to their poor lodgings, and went to bed noiselessly, for fear of awakening the suspicions of jealous or ill-disposed neighbors : it was still the reign of terror.

The family party in the Hôtel Lamartine at this time consisted of my grandfather and grandmother, who had borne him six children ; the eldest son, a man of great merit and ability, and of studious habits, who had shared his father's imprisonment, although holding himself advanced liberal opinions. But it was a wise, just, and moderate liberality, the natural result of his distinguished education. My grandfather could not endure the new law which had just then come into force, whereby this, his favorite and eldest son would share equally with his other children, instead of inheriting the whole of his property, as in former times. My grandmother, who had been born at Besançon, could not either accustom herself to the idea that he would only have his share, and that the others would "rob" him, as she called it, of that which was his right by birth, thanks to some unheard-of change in the civil code. The second son, the disciple and friend of M. de la Fayette, who had procured him a canonry, with the reversion to a bishopric, had not yet returned from the pontoons of Rochefort, although his release was momentarily expected. The third was my father, the Chevalier de Lamartine, who likewise had only just escaped from prison, and who had been married for two or three years. My grandfather had given him a nice little detached house for his wife and children, which communicated with the family mansion by a long covered passage. Three daughters, all nuns or *chanoinesses* — Mlle. de Lamartine, Mlle. de Villars, and Mlle. de Monceau — turned out of their convents by the Revolution, and obliged to seek a shelter in the home of their childhood, took care of their parents, with a timid and obedient tenderness which was touching to watch. At the top of the house, looking on the garden, was another apartment, occupied by a dear old aunt, the only sister of my grandfather, who was called Mlle. de Luzy. She had been for thirty years Superior of the Ursulines at Mâcon. Driven out of her convent, like all the rest, she had been received with open arms by my grandfather, and lived very happily in her retreat, in spite of her age and infirmities, and was carefully tended by one of her nuns, a sister named Nanette. My nurse used to carry me to her room regularly every day. Even to this hour I have an indelible recollection of these two women, who held a large place in my heart. Goodness is always fascinating to a child: holy faces, whether of children or of old people, have the same charm. It is the beauty and purity of childhood in both cases. Dear aunt Luzy! dear sister Nanette! before I knew what it was to feel, I loved you!

III.

I lived for several months in this way. Then came a day when I was startled by seeing my aunts in tears, and I was told to be very quiet, for my grandmother, who was upwards of eighty, had just died. My grandfather, who was also ill, had me brought and placed upon his bed to give me his last blessing. He had composed some pretty verses on my birth; I found them not long ago, in my mother's writing-table. He was very fond of me and so he kissed me tenderly, and gave me some bonbons. Little as I guessed it, this was our last parting: he died two or three days after. I see him still: he was a magnificent old man, with his high forehead, and soft, long, white hair. He had been one of the handsomest men of his time, when he was in the army, and when in garrison at Lille, under Louis XV., he had been a great favorite with Mlle. Clairon, who had just made her *début*, and was greatly struck by him. I have often seen the remains of his magnificent camp equipage, with its beautiful silver plate and silver warming-pan, and all the luxury of the young noblemen of his day. It was the bivouac of this reign; yet it did not diminish the valor of our troops at Fontenoy. Two of my uncles were killed by the English battery, and the third was knighted and received the Cross of St. Louis.

IV.

My grandfather being dead, the division of his property followed. It was a long and thorny task. The new law, abolishing primogeniture had scarcely been called into existence

The peasants, those sons of the soil, did not understand it; they felt it was contrary to their conscience, and so carried it out as inefficiently as possible. No lawyer could make the father of a family understand that he had not a right to deal as he pleased with his own property; and that by giving his eldest son the largest portion he thereby robbed the younger ones. An abstraction of right, or equality, has little chance of prevailing against nature.

My father was summoned to receive his share, but he never would consent to it. The habit of respecting the wishes and intentions of his father was to him a higher law than any written code. To profit by the new act would have seemed to him a positive sacrilege. He had received as a *dot* on his marriage a little property called Milly, worth about 250*l.* a year, and that sufficed for his humble wants. He declared that he was satisfied with this poor portion of my grandfather's magnificent inheritance, and renounced all further share. So he remained a poor man; but he won the love and admiration of the whole family. The rest of the property was divided by lot, which gave rise to long and painful discussions; but at last all was amicably settled. My eldest uncle and aunt, who were both unmarried, had the estate of Monceau and the vineyards in Champagne. My uncle, the Abbé Lamartine, had the Château of Ursy, in the midst of the forest of Burgundy, near Dijon. The house and gardens were magnificent, and the solitude complete. This suited my good old uncle, who would not, to please the Revolution, give up his priestly functions; but abjuring all society for the sake of peace, was content to live as a hermit according to his own convictions. I have always loved and venerated this uncle, who was a real St. Evremond in our family. When I grew older I was frequently his guest, and always happier with him than with any one else. Madame de Villars, the *chanoinesse*, who had made a vow of poverty, obtained a dispensation from the Pope, on the condition of being simply a distributor of her income, and became the proprietress of the rich property of Péronne, where she always lived in summer. She kept her promises to the Church with scrupulous fidelity, and became the generous benefactress of the whole neighborhood. She was handsome and clever, thoroughly versed in habits of business, and was of great use to my father on several occasions. Mlle. de Monceau, who had all her life been rather childish, lived with my father and mother. She was always treated as one of the children of the family, and by her large income added to the comfort and happiness of our home. The shares having been thus adjusted, every one went to take possession of his property. The Hôtel de Mâcon alone was kept as a common home for us all to pass the winter together.

V.

I was just beginning to see and understand something of outside things when my father and mother carried us off — a whole tribe of children, in a long file of bullock wagons — to establish us and all our worldly goods at Milly. Our dear mother was in the first carriage with two of my sisters on her knees, and another at her breast; a quantity of loose packages filled up the lumbering vehicle. My father went on foot as a sportsman, carrying his gun, cheering my mother, and helping the carriage when it got into any bad ruts. Two dogs in a leash followed him, and then two more wagons full of maids and nurses and household goods of every description, going at a foot's pace. Then came a carriage containing Mlle. de Monceau and her maid. All this formed a regular procession of old-fashioned equipages rolling and tumbling about in the mud, for the public roads in those days were execrable. The cries of the drivers, the lowing of the bullocks, the clamor and fright of the women servants, and the hearty laughter of the children at each fresh misfortune, made up a picturesque scene, which was partly amusing and partly touching. We did not arrive at Milly for five or six hours, although it was hardly more than twelve miles.

Milly was then a poor little village built on the ridge of a hill planted with vines, at some distance from St. Sorlin, which was the rural capital of the country.

VI.

Evei since the spring, my father had come to Milly from time to time to prepare the house for his family. The revolutionists had, to a certain degree, spared the old place, and contented themselves with turning the drawing-room into a dancing saloon on Sundays for the benefit of the neighboring peasantry. The sabots of the dancers had broken the old encaustic tiles into a thousand bits; not from pure mischief, but simply from a sort of pleasure at profaning a nobleman's house. We stumbled among the broken fragments of pavement until a workman had clumsily repaired it with large square common bricks. There was not much more damage done. The vines continued to bear and the fruit trees to blossom, so that the traces of the Revolution in Milly might be said to be restricted to the ball-room. Every one — father, mother, aunt, children, and servants — had soon found his or her place in the house. Our only furniture were a few beds, tables, and chairs. The kitchen, soon filled by the peasant women, once more sent up the cheerful smoke from its wide, ingle-nooked chimney. The nurse and children walked and played in the corridor. My father spent his days in hunting or shooting on the mountains. My mother was occupied in writing, in the care and superintendence of the house, or in visiting the sick and suffering, with whom she at once made friends, and was beloved as readily as she herself loved all around her.

VII.

Do you wish for a description ot these my first happy days at Milly? The account of one day will serve for all the rest.

No sooner had the first rays of the sun lit up my mother's room, than my father, who was a very early riser, went out walking. A maid used to fetch me and put me into my father's place, by the side of my darling, gentle mother, who used to kiss and pet me, and then teach me to lisp my little prayers. I did not know very well the meaning of the words, or understand what that Invisible and Omnipotent Power was, called

God; but I knew I was doing like mamma, and that was more than enough for me. Most good things are done from imitation. To try and be like what one loves, that is the first instinct of man. At any rate, it was mine. Reasoning one may dispute, but not that which has become a habit. My father was not a very religious, but he was an honest and an honorable man. The love and respect of his wife, whom he adored, made him pious almost in spite of himself.

After prayers we went to breakfast, I on my nurse's knee, off the vinedresser's soup, which I used to think the best in the world. Then I trotted off into the vineyards to play with my companions (the children of our peasants), or else, like them, to keep the goats and sheep in the mountain forests. We used to return when the bell of the old steeple rung the midday *Angelus*. Then a fuming hot soup with bacon and vegetables awaited us round the homely wooden table; a repast which I infinitely preferred to the pure white tablecloth and more delicate dishes served to my parents. I remember even now with appetite the little two-pronged, two-penny forks which doubled into our pocket clasped-knives, and with which we used to pick out and eat the bouilli of our soup, in little bright red or green varnished earthenware bowls! Soup has ever since appeared a luxury to me. A cabbage or celery leaf, with a radish, just stirred in what is called "tea-kettle broth," with a bit of black bread, this is the true food of the country peasant. My simple life made me relish the homely fare of the cottager as much as a child who had known nothing else. When I grew older, and was no longer allowed to run wild, and the age of lessons and school came, I was obliged to give up this simple food of goat's cheese, cabbage, onions, and the like, and made to eat meat, which disagreed with me so much that I had a regular illness in consequence; and, ever since, I have never lost the early tastes contracted at that time. Even when we dined up-stairs, my mother never could persuade us to eat anything but vegetables.

After dinner, my father used to go back to his shooting on the mountains, sometimes alone, at other times in company with one of his head vinedressers, of whom he had made both a guide and friend. This man, who was in every way superior to his class, was called Claude Chanut, and became quite a favorite with us all.

VIII.

Sometimes it happened that we passed the whole winter at Milly, as in a kind of domestic convent, completely snowed up, but visited from time to time by certain old friends of my father's, who were living in hiding, as it were, in the neighboring villages. First, there was the doctor of the canton, who lived with his wife at St. Sorlin, with a son, who became my great friend, and a daughter, whom I should have fallen in love with, if I had been of the right age. Then there was the Chevalier de La Cense, a retired officer in the Guards, living with his sister, Mademoiselle de Moleron, in the same village, a cheery, jovial, good-natured man, whose arrival brightened the whole house. Then there was M. de Vaudran, of the Bruys family (one of twenty children, all distinguished in their different careers), living at Bussières, in the parish of Milly. M. de Vaudran, who was an old friend of my father's, had been secretary to M. de Villedeuil before the Revolution, and initiated into all the political secrets of the highest society in Paris. He was a Royalist of the good old school — moderate, impartial, and just towards every one, even towards the men who had mingled in the Revolution, without having imbrued their hands in crime and blood. He took pity on my somewhat neglected education, and gave me my first writing-lessons on a little table in the dining-room, for which I have remained eternally grateful to him. His three sisters — simple, gentle, loving, agreeable women, and great friends of my mother's — often accompanied him to Milly. Although obliged, from political circumstances, to live continually in the country, and only associate with people of a humbler class, the natural distinction of their manners, and the companionship of their brother, who always spent part of the year with them, gave them a high-bred tone which could not be mistaken; and their entire absence of affectation made their reception of friends in their own home most pleasant; while their natural grace and dignity gave a special charm to their conversation.

The Curé de Bussières, their near neighbor, young, handsome, mundane, amiable, and of elegant and refined habits, was full of respect and deference for these ladies, and he was also a favorite shooting companion of my father's.

IX.

At a quarter of a league from our house, buried in the wooded gorges of the mountains of St. Point, was a site which has enshrined itself in my memory and imagination forever. I mean the village and château of Pierreclos — the habitation of the old Count de Pierreclos, whom I have before mentioned. Walter Scott has nothing more romantic or original in his descriptions of the nature, habits, and dwelling-places of the Scotch lairds. Now for a description of the château itself, its inmates, and the life they led there.

We used to go and dine there every Sunday after high mass; that is, at a quarter before twelve. After having clambered on foot to the summit of the Csaz mountain, which threw a long gray shadow over the Milly valley behind my father's garden, a steep and rapid descent to the right brought us into the Pierreclos valley. A rough path, full of rolling stones, but shaded by old walnut-trees, led us by several barren hamlets to the head of the valley. There the aspect of the scenery changes; the hills, covered with vineyards, slope down towards the rich meadows, irrigated by bright and rushing streams, and shaded by poplars cutting the sky-line, like the cypresses of the South. Very soon the valley widens, and the eye is lost in a distant vapory forest of pines and beech. The background is formed of dark mountains, covered here and there with snow, which lies in deep patches in the hollows. After having walked on a little way on the high-road, we used to perceive a mass of smoke and vapor coming out of the mouths of the village furnaces, which blackened even the walls of the old steeple of Pierreclos. But it was church time, and we hurried into the chapel, where the priest was saying mass. The old lord and his family occupied a bench to the right of the altar. The family consisted of the master of the château, a gouty old man, but with a proud and determined countenance, who looked down with a sort of insolence on his old vassals; his brother, M. de Berzé, who bore the name of the old Gothic château of which we spoke just now, between Milly and Cluny; his five daughters, all very pleasing-looking, both in face and figure; and a young son, of about the same age as myself, with whom hereafter I was to be bound in the ties of a warm friendship. As soon as we appeared they made room for us in the church, and we were soon kneeling in our proper seats. The mass being over, the peasants separated. The old lord mounted his horse (with the help of his servants), and rode up to the castle by a steep paved road. We followed on foot with the rest of the family, and winding through the vineyards, soon arrived at the iron gates of the château. Nothing could be more imposing than its appearance as you entered. A vast courtyard, which led you through a high subterranean passage, or covered way, to the keep, from which you suddenly emerged into an open sunny space brilliant with flowers, growing up to the very foot of the steeple of the old chapel, which was built on a high terrace to the extreme left of the castle. Then the ground suddenly fell, like a drop-scene in the opera, and revealed to you a mass of towers and pinnacles and quaint Gothic windows and ornaments, the whole lit up and illuminated, as it were, by the setting sun.

X.

On first entering the large courtyard, I was struck at the sight of a new building not yet finished, on the windows of which the workmen, in fact, were still at work. It was evidently intended to replace the old Gothic castle, which, being mainly composed of keeps and square towers, circular staircases, irregular turrets, and pointed roofs, was more picturesque than comfortable, and rather gave one the idea of an aerial village. This old fortress, in reality, had been built on the edge of a promontory, and followed the sinuosities of the rock both above and below, from the summit to the valley. The upper part formed an oval terrace, upon which all the doors opened, whether of the kitchens or drawing-rooms.

XI.

The apartments with the exception of a great stove in an angle of the dining-room, and a magnificent fire-place of black marble in the drawing-room, large enough to burn whole trees at a time, had the appearance of rooms recently restored after a fire of the day before. The mortar scarcely filled up the spaces between the stones; and the walls, guiltless of whitewash, seemed never to have been smoothed by the mason's trowel. The flames had licked the paint off the ceilings, which bore the traces of an incendiary fire, seemingly scarcely put out.

"Look!" exclaimed the old Count, showing me the marks of the above-mentioned destruction; "look at the traces of the passage of those brigands! Here was the torch of one, there the hatchet of another, a pickaxe was the tool of the third. Ah! the rascals! I know them well; and never in my lifetime will I suffer the remembrance of these horrors to be effaced."

In truth in 1790, in the famous and inexplicable day called *du Brigandage*, this grand old castle had been completely ravaged, and nearly burnt to the ground, by the peasants from the mountains, who had determined to avenge the supposed wrongs of the villagers, and took advantage of the unpopularity of the owner, who was hated by the people, to carry out their nefarious designs. The pillage and devastation were indeed complete.

His wife and daughters were saved by the fidelity of two or three of their tenant farmers, and concealed in the neighboring forest. The Count and his son escaped by a miracle, and swore to be avenged. His eldest son emigrated the next day. As to the old Count himself, he returned after a time to his ruined home, and went on living there till the day when they came to carry off the cannons of his terrace to Mâcon, at the same time that his whole family were thrown into prison by the agents of the Revolutionary government. My father, who in 1790 was on leave at Monceau, armed and mounted the young men of Mâcon, and pursued the incendiaries to the Château of Cormatin, killing several in an engagement in the neighborhood of Cluny, and hanging others on the trees by the roadside, — a service never forgotten in the grateful memory of the old Count. The insurrection was at an end, and order was everywhere restored, until the day when the Government, in its turn, had given the signal for persecution, and imprisoned, as we have said, the whole family as Royalists.

XII.

The head of the family had been formerly captain of cavalry during the Seven Years' War. He had been taken prisoner by the Prussians, and used to tell us how the Queen of Prussia, delighted with his good looks and cleverness, used to knock every morning at his door in the corridor, calling out, "Count Pierreclos! get up, and follow the King's hunting party! Your horses are waiting." "At these words," he added, "I gladly rose, and started for Sans Souci, where we used to eat delicious sour-krout." The Queen of Prussia was always brought into the conversation.

On returning from Potsdam, he sent in his resignation, and married a young girl of good family from the neighborhood of Lyons. She bore him five or six children, and they lived constantly in the Château of Pierreclos, the old Count being the object of the timid fear of the peasantry, and the ridicule of the middle classes. He was not a bad man at all, but absurdly vain and boastful, with a good heart at bottom, though often violent and rough in his manners. His wife had died during their imprisonment. The eldest of his sons had emigrated; the youngest who was called the Chevalier de Pierreclos, was a boy of my own age, brave, clever, and intelligent, left to nature and with scarcely any education; but giving promise of what he afterwards became — a brilliant adventurer, like the

Chevalier de Grammont, a hero of the civil wars, of romantic love affairs, of duels, horses, and all that is comprehended in the old term of a "free lance." We were intimate from children, and shared in all boyish sports.

His sisters, older than himself, were handsome, *piquante*, and original. As they had no mother, they had consequently little or no education, properly so called; they, in fact, brought up one another. There was certainly in the château an old aunt, the only sister of the Count, a clever woman, and as strange as himself; but who could only have taught cards to her pretty nieces, that being the one occupation of Madame de Moirode from morning till night. She used to come into the drawing-room at eight o'clock in the morning, and sit on a curtained seat, like Madame du Deffant! Then lowering the curtains round her on three sides, to keep out the draught, she would offer cards to all comers: brothers, sisters, nephews, nieces, friends — no matter who! playing without a moment's intermission from one meal to another; resting for a few minutes, perhaps, in the middle of the day, and beginning again with any new-comers till supper-time.

The Chevalier de Berzé, an old cavalry officer like his brother, the Count de Pierreclos, ran through his whole fortune very early in life, and now had accepted the posts of agent and gardener to the family. In the drawing-room his only functions seemed to be to provide fresh cards, and to bring in fresh logs for the fire. He was a thoroughly good-natured, "serviceable" fellow, ready to do a kind turn to everybody, and universally beloved. I saw him live, grow old, and die, like a living piece of furniture, having no idea in life but that of saying "Yes" to everything proposed by his brother; of bringing the finest melons from the garden to the dining-room, the most beautiful flowers to his nieces, and fresh faggots for the inexhaustible fire-places in both apartments.

XIII.

But when the time of the vintage drew near, everything assumed an aspect of work and life and gayety, which metamorphosed the whole country. The peasants loaded their carts with water thoroughly to cleanse the deep wine-presses which were to hold the grapes. The bullocks, coupled together and harnessed at dawn, lifted their intelligent heads and velvety eyes under the heavy yoke; or else ruminated, by the side of the pole, the armfuls of hay which the children gave them. The women, lifting us up in their arms, would help us to scramble up by the axle of the wheels into the vat. This was a large, oval kind of bath, in which the vine-dresser goes to the vineyard, and which he there fills with great bunches of cut grapes to bring them back to the wine-press. Then we were lifted out by the workmen, and our places filled by the contents of their baskets. A quantity of sticky flies and wasps, drunk with the juice of the grape which had already begun to ferment, fell with the fruit into the vat, but either instinct or satiety prevented their stinging us.

Thus we went joyfully from one vine to the other, helping to cut the rich bunches and fill the baskets or bins of one set of reapers after the other. The cleverest and handiest girls from the neighboring villages formed themselves into bands, slept in the barn at Milly, and were hired as cutters by the owners of the vineyards. They used to walk singing, their pails on their heads, or their baskets on their arms, behind the one who served as guide in the narrow paths between the vines; and then placing themselves by twenties or thirties, each at the foot of a vine stock, would quickly clear the whole stem with careful, skillful hands, of its rich white or blue burden, squash them in their fingers, and throw them into the bins, which the boys would then carry off to the carts. The very vineyards seemed to sing as their rich produce fell under the scissors; the earth, as it were, rejoiced at her spoil. We, children, used to follow the carts dripping with their juicy burden; our little pinafores all stained with the blood of the grape, and meeting with joyous cries each fresh band of workers. The joy ran like the wine from hill to hill. Then we helped to empty the grapes from the vat to the wine-press; or gathered bunches of fresh grapes to refresh the tired bullocks, whose carts creaked under their heavy load. Then we would count the number of bins, and run to tell our father, who would calculate the numbers of tuns of wine which would be the final result, and which, in reality, formed our whole income for the year. A few days after, the same work was begun again, until the leaves of the vine, all yellow and seared, had no more fruit to conceal; until, in fact, the vintage being over and the barrels filled to the brim with wine, the vines were left desolate, the goats picked off the few remaining leaves, and the once busy paths were still as death.

XIV.

Then began the spinning of the flax and hemp in the evenings at home; or else the cracking of the walnuts, which was the last gay work of the season for the villagers. The mistress of the house, by the light of a rustic lamp called a *creuse-yeux*, gathered round the large kitchen table, children, servants, visitors, and neighbors. The men went to the cellar and brought out huge sacks of nuts, of which the husk, already half rotten, was easily detached from the shell, and threw them on the floor. Every one, armed with a hammer, set to work on a heap of this rich fruit before him, to crack the nuts carefully, and take out the kernel (if possible entire) and put them in little heaps, either for sale or for the oil mill. Gay laughter and innocent conversation echoed from one end of the room to the other, and made the work seem like play. When all was done, dancing began, and generally continued till midnight.

It was the same with the weaving of the hemp and flax, which used to occupy the winter evenings in the great barn until the tow merchant came round and bargained for the long hanks of yarn and vegetable silk, the produce of which was the gain of the wives and daughters and women-servants of the house, and often served to keep them in clothes altogether. We used to take our share in all these works with our servants and peasants, as was the custom in those primitive days. The presence of our gentle mother was a check on any light or im-

Milton Keynes UK
Ingram Content Group UK Ltd.
UKHW012249290324
440241UK00004B/228

9 783385 384149